CANARY RED

CANARY RED

by

ROBERT McKAY

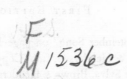

MEREDITH PRESS/*New York*

Library of Congress Catalog Card Number: 68–26336

Manufactured in the United States of America
for MEREDITH PRESS

TO THE LOSERS—MAY THEY ALL
BECOME WINNERS

CANARY RED

CHAPTER ONE

They had to wait supper half an hour for Uncle George, which was unusual, and then when he gunned his old Pontiac up the rutty driveway and ran over Sara's hydrangea bush they didn't have to get within sniffing distance to know he'd been in conference at the Lakeview Inn.

"I suppose you've got the old red carpet all cleaned and ready to roll out," he said loudly, scowling at Sara and Ming.

"I'll red carpet you, George Peabody, if you don't get out there and tie up my hydrangea bush!"

George ignored her.

"All ready for the prodigal's return, aren't we!" He glanced around the kitchen as if expecting to see a couple of fatted calves tucked away in a corner.

At his best Uncle George was no joy to Ming Campbell. Tall and bulky, but without strength or grace or dignity, he filled his clothes the way water fills a plastic sack. He had thick sticky brown hair and small, round, too-personal eyes that kept flicking at you . . . flick . . . flick . . . flick . . . as though trying to discover how much you knew about him.

He was a great talker, drunk or sober, and a great schemer-dreamer. Unfortunately (or perhaps fortunately, Sara was never sure which), he lacked the daring and the single-mindedness of the successful entrepreneur. He would make a start, and when things got tight he would borrow a little money—but when things got really tight, when the situation called for total commitment, George would invariably waver. Trying to fish and cut bait at the same time, he usually ended up with half a bucket of perch while somebody else went home with the bass and muskellunge.

But at least he did come home with the perch, Sara often consoled herself. And maybe someday—if he kept going out on the water—maybe someday an addled muskellunge would jump right into his boat. Which was actually what George Peabody wanted and expected.

"I was talking to Bert Bradley," George said as they sat down to eat in the big old-fashioned dining room. This was one farm where nobody ate in the kitchen. The kitchen was small, strictly a workshop. The dining room was the biggest room in the house, and cluttered with glass-fronted cabinets in which Ming Campbell's grandmother had displayed her painted plates and china sugar bowls that looked like tomatoes and butter dishes that looked like lobsters. The stuff was still there—some of it ugly, some not so ugly. And if Sara suspected it might be worth money, she kept this opinion to herself.

"Bert Bradley tells me Mason Campbell's got a pretty

4

bad reputation, Ming. I reckon you know that by now."

Ming kept her eyes on her plate.

"There's no need to go into that," Sara said tartly. "Ming and I've been through the whole thing and there's no need to hash it all over again."

"Bert tells me Mason Campbell better walk pretty close to the line or he may find himself right back where he came from."

"George!"

"Bert says Mason Campbell's got a pile of money hid away somewhere. Much as two hundred thousand dollars." George sucked his teeth.

"Now George, that's all a lot of nonsense! Bert Bradley's got no business——"

"They're gonna be watching him," George said. "But if he's careful he'll be all right. Man with that kind of money oughtn't to worry himself too much about a little old farm like this, now had he?"

"Are you going to meet his train, Uncle George?"

"Meet his train?" George's little round eyes peered suspiciously at Ming. "Why should I meet his train?"

"I don't know—I thought you might want to get on the good side of him."

"Now just a minute, young lady!" George pulled his eyebrows down the way he did when he thought he had a chance to intimidate somebody. Ming stared back at him innocently.

"He's your father and all that," George blustered. "But he's also an ex-convict and I think you might do well to keep that in mind. Personally I can't see myself buttering up to no ex-convict." He paused, frowning at Ming.

"But on the other hand we gotta be fair, and the fair thing is to give the man the benefit of the doubt." He nodded, plainly impressed by what he had said. "I believe I *will* meet that train. Might do Mason a world of good to see a friendly face waiting for him."

George lit one of his fat brown cigars. "You better ride in along with me, Ming," he said, blowing smoke expansively. "Your daddy'll be wanting to see you first thing, and I think it's the least we can do. Give him a good friendly welcome and let him know we're willing to let bygones be bygones."

"Oh, I don't think so. . . ." The last thing she wanted was to sit in the car, at the station, with people staring at her.

"W-e-l-l-l," George said, drawing the word out. "You're mighty free with advice to your elders—but if it was me and it was my daddy coming home, I think I'd want to be right there when he got off the train so he'd know I loved him and wanted him back."

Uncle George could surprise you occasionally. He was sneaky sly, and sometimes he could put his stupid finger on the exact spot that hurt the most.

No more was said about it, but the next day as three o'clock approached, Ming was getting ready to ride into town with Uncle George. She agonized over what to wear. She couldn't go in jeans and blouse, that was for sure. And she didn't want to dress up too much, either. She compromised, finally, by dressing as she would for school—and then *that* didn't feel right; made her feel as though she *was* going to school.

6

"Why don't you just wear your blue cotton dress," Aunt Sara said helpfully. And the wonder was that this time she was perfectly right.

They reached the station a few minutes early, and for once Uncle George seemed content to sit quietly in the car instead of getting out and looking around for someone to talk to. And there were plenty of people to talk to, Ming saw with dismay. They were all shooting glances sideways at George and Ming, but nobody approached the car directly; and in a strange way none of them seemed quite willing to acknowledge openly that they even knew George and Ming.

George shifted uncomfortably in his seat. He stared straight ahead. Ming felt herself tottering on the edge of panic. She had known the town would be curious, but she hadn't expected anything like *this*. Suppose her father was drunk or something when he got off the train! Or suppose he was all wrinkled and old from the years in prison—and maybe his mind wouldn't be quite right and he'd stare around, bewildered, and then the people would laugh at him. . . .

Her father. And the wildest, craziest, funniest, saddest, most mind-staggering thing about her father's homecoming was that up until twenty-four hours ago she hadn't even known she *had* a father. A real live flesh-and-blood father, that is.

She had been weeding carrots in the garden, yesterday, and Aunt Sara had called her into the kitchen and sat her down and told her to hold on to herself now and just listen and not get all excited.

Aunt Sara was the one who ought to hold on to herself, Ming had been thinking. Aunt Sara was a big solid woman with soft firm skin and short frizzy blond hair that didn't show the gray. When she was excited her face turned rosy, and sweat popped out in little beads and sometimes ran in rivulets down the folds of her plump pink neck.

"I don't know how to tell it," Aunt Sara had said, shaking her head hopelessly. Her glasses steamed up and she had to take them off and polish them on her apron.

Ming waited. It was actually cool in the kitchen after the loamy heat of the new garden. And although farm work was not one of the things she liked best in the world, she had found that the easiest way to take care of the garden was to do it alone. Because when Uncle George helped he stood around mostly, with a cigar in his mouth, telling her what she was doing wrong. And when Aunt Sara helped it was worse, because Aunt Sara, so nimble in her kitchen, was like a cow with blind staggers in the garden. She stepped on the radishes and knelt on the asparagus and when she got a hoe in her hand you might as well kiss half your corn crop good-bye.

But now Aunt Sara was fishing a limp envelope out of her apron pocket. "I knew it would come someday," she said, "but I hoped it would be another few years yet, when you were older and it wouldn't be such a shock and all." She fanned herself with the letter. "I'd rather take a whipping with harness leather than tell you this, Ming, and that's the truth of it."

"Tell me *what?*" Ming thought it probably had to do with Uncle George. He was always getting his tail caught in somebody's wringer. Like the time he took

8

an option on those lake front lots. He had actually gone to work in the factory at Marion for a while after that one. Aunt Sara's credit had been cut off, and she had said she couldn't hardly hold her head up when she went to town anymore.

"Well, Ming, this is going to be awful hard for you to understand. But the fact is we never told you the truth about your daddy."

Ming sat absolutely still. She looked past Aunt Sara at the chipped yellowing enamel of the refrigerator door.

"Maybe we should have, I don't know. It was your grandpa who decided we shouldn't, and he made me take a solemn oath I'd never tell you till you were out of school."

Uncle George had bought the refrigerator secondhand. The motor made a clicking noise like somebody holding a stick against the spokes of a bicycle wheel every time it started up.

"Your daddy didn't die in the war, Ming. He's alive and he's coming home."

"Coming home?"

"He'll be here tomorrow." Aunt Sara caught her breath. "Honey, he's . . . he's been in prison. All this time. And now he's getting out."

"In *prison*?" That couldn't be. Her father was a picture on her dressing table. A laughing man—a boy, really—gazing straight at you out of the picture. Laughing. A wide reckless mouth. His hair blowing in the wind.

"Your daddy got in trouble," Aunt Sara said, "back in nineteen forty-six, right after the war. It was down south.

And when he went to prison, your mother didn't have anyone to turn to except your grandfather, so he brought her up here to live."

"But didn't anybody around here *know?*"

"Nobody knew. That's how come your grandpa to make up the story Mason had died in England. Later years he sometimes wondered if he had done right, but at the time it just seemed best to him if you could grow up here in Blairsville without any scandal." Sara sighed. "Your poor momma was sick the whole time she carried you, and after you were born she just withered away. That's when your grandpa asked me and George if we would come live here on the farm—he was alone, you see, and he didn't know much about taking care of little baby girls."

Sara pushed her lips in and out and then got up and went to the sink and fixed herself an Alka-Seltzer. "Your grandpa told me the whole story first day I was here. But he never did cotton much to your uncle George, and he made me promise I wouldn't tell George. My own husband . . . But your grandpa had the right idea, and George wouldn't know to this day if the old man hadn't passed away. Which of course was the one thing he never counted on—he figured he'd be right here to tell you when the time came."

"Oh, I don't know!" Ming cried. "I just can't seem to *believe* it."

Sara's mouth twitched nervously. She drank the rest of the Alka-Seltzer and took a long time rinsing the glass.

"I don't even *know* him, Aunt Sara. How can I feel like he's my father?"

10

Sara moved quickly across the kitchen and put her hand on the girl's trembling shoulder. Ming didn't look up. Sara gave her shoulder a little squeeze, then pulled her chair closer and sat herself firmly down, knee to knee with the young girl.

"I don't have any easy answers for you, honey. My own thought was that he shouldn't come home—not yet. But you see, Ming, this is really his place since your grandpa died, and I can't very well tell him not to come."

"*His* place?"

"Yes. That was a shock, too, let me tell you. We were expecting, naturally, that the farm would go to you, with us probably to take care of it till you came of age. But the lawyer called me and George into his office and read us the will in private, because the old man had left the whole kit and caboodle to Mason, and at that time me and the lawyer were the only ones who knew Mason was still alive.

"Well, George almost had a stroke right then and there. He hadn't hardly ever even heard of Mason Campbell. But it was all explained in the will—the old man said he thought twenty years was enough punishment for any crime, and he wanted Mason to know the farm was there waiting for him when he got out."

Aunt Sara's businesslike demeanor suddenly deserted her and she began to cry. "I've just *begged* Mason not to come back here. I wrote him and told him to think of you and what this would do to you. He wrote back a real nice letter, I'll say that for him. He's sorry it will inconvenience us, but he claims he's got his plans laid out and the farm is part of it."

11

Sara took off her glasses and wiped her eyes. "Like as not he'll sell the place and move to the city. From what I've heard about him, he's not the type of man to settle down and farm it for the rest of his life."

"Well, we'll just see about that!" Ming said indignantly. "He's not going to come back here and ruin all our lives!"

"It's his place, Ming. He can do whatever he likes with it as soon as he's out of prison."

"It's not *fair!* Even if he *is* my father. All these years he hasn't done a darn thing but sit in a prison, and now he can come home and own everything like he was a hero or something."

"Now, now. That won't do any good, Ming. But I'll admit it's hard not to feel that way," she added uncomfortably. "Course the farm isn't much of a farm anymore. Your grandpa had to sell so much land to keep us going while he was sick. But a real goer could make something of it, even now."

Sara was breathing heavily. "George is going to find out a thing or two, I'm afraid, and I don't look forward to it. I just hope him and Mason can get along, but from what I've heard of your father I kind of doubt it."

"Don't you *know* him?"

"I never laid eyes on him. He enlisted in the Canadian Army when he was sixteen and was shipped to England. That's when he met your mother. And in forty-two, after America entered the war, they let him transfer to the United States Army."

"You know, it's funny I never thought about it before, but you and Grandpa never even told me what he did in the war. And I guess I never asked."

12

"You used to ask," Sara said ruefully. "And ask and ask and ask. But your grandpa didn't want to talk about Mason, not even the good things, so I guess you finally got discouraged."

"The *good* things?"

Sara bit her lip. For a moment Ming thought she wasn't going to answer. Then, without a word, she left the kitchen, and Ming could hear her climbing the stairs and opening bureau drawers. She was panting when she returned, but smiling now and rosy-faced.

"Well, you make me awfully ashamed, Ming. Because there were some good things—a lot of good things." She handed Ming two small flat leather boxes. "It's a pity. All those years up there in the dark where nobody could see them."

Ming opened one of the boxes. Inside was a tarnished medal hanging on a ribbon.

"That's the Silver Star," Sara said. "Your father won it in Normandy."

Ming, hands suddenly trembling, opened the other box.

"That's the Distinguished Service Cross," Sara said. "Not many soldiers ever won that medal, Ming. General Eisenhower himself pinned it on your daddy."

A surging pride, sharp and fierce as the Silver Star, welled up inside Ming and caught her by the throat.

"But he really was a hero then. He really was."

"Yes. For a little while. Till he robbed that bank."

"Robbed a *bank!* Is that what he did?"

"That's what he did."

"*Why?* Why would he do a thing like that?"

Sara lifted her shoulders. "Why would anybody? For

money, I guess. And Mason was always wild—your grandfather told me—even in the Army. He'd be a sergeant one day and a private the next, for insulting an officer or something.

"When he got out he didn't know anything, except soldiering, which was a drug on the market in nineteen forty-six. So he couldn't make the kind of money he wanted. And then he had this violent temper, and whenever he did find a job his boss would usually turn out to be some fat cat who had made his pile while Mason and the other boys were doing the fighting. Mason wasn't too good at taking orders anyway—and pretty soon there'd be a flare-up and Mason would get fired.

"Your grandfather told me this. He wasn't excusing Mason, understand—he was just telling me what kind of a hothead Mason was in those days." Sara paused and pursed her lips. "Course there was plenty of other young hotheads in the same boat, but not very many of them ever set out to rob a bank."

"At least he . . . he had *some* good in him," Ming said, surprised to find herself defending Mason Campbell. She wasn't thinking of him as her father. She was thinking of a twenty-two-year-old stranger back from the wars with two medals and a pregnant wife and an empty wallet. And maybe having to beg somebody like Uncle George for a job!

"Sure he had some good in him," Sara said. "In the beginning your grandfather used to get to feeling awful bad sometimes, and then he'd tell me stories about Mason, or Mase, as he always called him. He'd go down to see him every year or so, but they couldn't write back and forth for fear somebody would find out—which in this town, with Milly Ferguson in the post office, somebody surely would have.

"Remember how he used to say he was going to the doctor up in Battle Creek? Well, that's when he'd go to Florida. And when he came back he'd be looking better than if he *had* been to Battle Creek. The last time he went down there—you were about seven, I guess—he came home real excited. Told me Mason was doing fine and was busy with a brand-new career. A new career for a man doing twenty years didn't make much sense to me, but after the will was read I realized it was probably right then he decided to leave the farm to Mason."

"You keep saying twenty years," Ming said. "But I'm only *fifteen*."

"Well, his sentence was twenty years. You see, your daddy and this other man stuck up a big bank and got away with eighty thousand dollars. But they didn't get very far. At least your daddy didn't. He had the gun, a machine gun it was, and the other man had the bag of money. Well, the police were right behind them and shooting at them as they ran to their car. But your daddy never made it. The police bullets hit him in the legs and shoulder and he fell in the street, and the man with the money just kept running and jumped in the car and got clean away.

"Your grandfather told me all this. And then, believe it or not, I read the whole thing in one of those true detective magazines—bought it right in Busby's Luncheonette not five years ago. But nobody in this town seemed to connect the name, and the picture of Mason was so

dark you couldn't see who it was. The detective magazine wrote it up because the police never did catch the
other man and the bank never got their money back."

"My father wouldn't tell who he was?"

"No, he wouldn't tell," Sara said disapprovingly. "And
if you ask me, he was plain crazy. Your grandfather used
to plead with him to tell. Because, you see, that's what
made it so hard on him. Being a war hero and all, he
probably wouldn't have got any twenty-year sentence if
he had turned state's evidence, I think they call it. Besides, he didn't shoot the machine gun and that was in
his favor. But the bank wanted their money back, and
when your daddy wouldn't help them they did everything
they could—which is considerable, believe me—to keep
him in prison for life. Why, he could have had a parole
back in fifty-one if he had just told them who the other
man was. But he wouldn't tell. And so he had to do all
his sentence except the time off for good behavior, and I
guess even the bank couldn't take that away from him."

"I never heard of such a thing!" Ming was outraged.
"That other man just left him lying there in the street and
ran off with the money. He *deserved* to be tattled on!"

"Yes." Her aunt smiled. "Your daddy may be a bank
robber, but he's sure no tattletale."

"I don't think that's very funny."

"No." Aunt Sara looked apologetic.

Ming was bouncing back. She was beginning to see a
ray of light. . . . If nobody in town knew about her
father, why did they have to find out now? Why couldn't
her father say——

But it was just then that Sheriff Sam Dunbar's souped-

16

up black Ford came growling into the yard, and Ming's ray of light went immediately out.

Sara and Ming had known the sheriff for a long time—what with the various foreclosures and quitclaims he periodically, and politely, left at the farmhouse for Uncle George's attention. He was portly and red-faced, and he smoked large cigars in true sheriff fashion, but behind the cigar was a very nice man, Ming had always thought.

This time, though, he was brusque—maybe because he thought he was bringing bad news. Then, when he found out they already knew Mason Campbell was coming home, he softened. Took his big gray Stetson hat off and mopped his forehead. "It's the damnedest thing I ever heard of," he said. "I shouldn't be telling you this —especially you." He looked at Ming. "But it's a small county and you're my friends, and I just can't run things the way the city cops do."

They waited, moving close to each other for support.

"Anyway, Bert Bradley saw it come in on the Teletype, and there ain't a chance in the world of keeping it quiet now. Bert's got a tongue like a swivel-jointed bell clapper."

"They still want the money, don't they?" Ming asked, half resentfully.

"I don't think so," the sheriff said, feeling his way. "Statute of limitations has run out on the robbery—but the FBI is still interested in that other fella. And the trouble is . . ." The sheriff hesitated. "Now I don't want to get you upset, but what come in on the wire said that Mason Campbell might be interested in that other fella, too."

"I shouldn't wonder," Sara said.

"And there's a chance the other fella might be interested in Mase," the sheriff added reluctantly. "The point is, we don't know just what kind of a situation might develop out of this."

Sara's eyes widened. "Oh, Lord!" She sat down abruptly in an old wicker rocker. "You ought to give us some protection, Sam."

"Oh, I don't look for any real trouble." The sheriff glanced at Ming. "And I haven't got the men, anyway, Sara. But you keep your eyes open. And if you see any strangers—or anything else you don't like—just give me a call and I'll be out here aflyin'."

When the sheriff left, Ming went back to her garden. She inspected the tomato vines, pulled a few suckers off the staked plants, then sat down on her heels between two hills of melons she had planted against Uncle George's pontifical advice. She idly turned the tender young leaves, looking for cucumber beetles.

What would he be like? She knew he wouldn't look the same, and he wouldn't *be* the same either, not after fifteen years.

Maybe he just made a mistake, she thought.

The trouble was, holding up a bank wasn't just a mistake. She could understand how a man might be tempted to steal, under certain circumstances—but holding up a *bank,* with a machine gun! No, he had been a dangerous and violent man fifteen years ago, and now, coming out of prison, he might be worse.

She shivered.

She was going to have a father, after all these years of Uncle George. But what kind of a father? An ex-convict was bad enough. A bank robber. But how about a crazy man? And a man would have to be crazy, she thought, to spend ten extra years in prison rather than inform on the very person who had put him there in the first place.

What would Billy Gabriel say? And Miss Dean? She dreaded the thought of facing the kids again, answering the unasked questions.

And always, all the time she was thinking these things, there was another thought way back in her mind. It just sat back there, patiently, as if it knew she would eventually have to bring it out and examine it. She didn't want to, though. And then she relaxed for an instant and the thought leaped into the forepart of her mind, crowding everything else to the corners.

What if he doesn't like *me?*

Yes. Such a funny thought. The world had suddenly swapped ends.

She rubbed her eyes with the back of her hand. And sweat got in her eyes. And it smarted and she started to cry. For the first time. Really cry. The tears dropped on the melon plant and rolled right down the trough of the leaves. The melon doesn't know teardrops from raindrops, she thought, and doesn't care either. Somehow it made her feel better. The world was going right on about its business. The melon vines were looking for water, and the cucumber beetles were looking for melon vines, and she was looking for cucumber beetles.

And somewhere between here and Florida her father was riding a train, and what he was looking for God only knew.

CHAPTER TWO

But now, sitting in the car with Uncle George, waiting for the train, Ming's stomach was knotted tight with apprehension.

And then she heard the blare of the Diesel's horn, a murmur from the curious crowd of townspeople, and now the train was sliding smoothly to a stop and there wasn't a sound. Not a sound.

George blew out his breath audibly. He opened his door, and Ming opened hers, and they stood together in front of the car—a big frightened man and a slim frightened girl.

There was only one passenger coach. The conductor poked his head out and looked up and down the track. Then he closed the door again. Nobody got off the train.

Ming looked at Uncle George. He shrugged. Like a man who has just learned that the dentist won't be able to see him until tomorrow.

But then, two cars down, almost at the end of the platform, Ming saw a tall wide-shouldered man in a gray suit leaping in and out of a baggage car, unloading dozens of cardboard boxes. Two of the trainmen were helping. One of them grinned and said something to the man in the gray suit. He shook his head silently. He wasn't grinning. His face was very dark, but Ming was too far away to see what he looked like.

"Could that be him?"

"How do I know!" Uncle George was getting nervous again.

The crowd had noticed now, and some of the bolder spirits moved down the platform toward the baggage car. Ming and Uncle George followed slowly.

"It's him!" A teen-age boy had sauntered bravely right up to the pile of boxes and read a shipping tag. "Mason Campbell!" The boy's eyes picked Ming out of the crowd. She could feel her face burning, but she stared back at him defiantly until he looked away.

The man in the gray suit unloaded his last armload of boxes, waved a casual good-bye to the baggagemen, and turned slowly to face the crowd. He was very tall, taller than Uncle George—and for a moment Ming felt there must be some mistake. He didn't look that tall in the old picture. But it was because his shoulders were so wide, she realized—the picture was only from the waist up and gave no hint of his immensely long straight legs.

No wonder I'm such a gangly thing, Ming thought.

She raised her eyes to his face.

He was watching the crowd. His face was still. There was no sign of the reckless good-natured grin that had greeted Ming every morning of her life from the picture frame on the dressing table. He had black careless hair, shaggy at the neck. His mouth was wide, firm—almost hard. His head was set very strongly on his shoulders —you noticed that, Ming thought, the high unyielding way he held his head. But what you noticed first, and remembered always, were his eyes. Under thick arched black brows his eyes were bright silver-blue. In the deeply tanned face they glittered like mirrors. He looked straight at the crowd. He was wary, and puzzled. His eyes were narrow, but they weren't defiant and they weren't afraid and they certainly weren't apologetic.

Ming felt something huge swelling inside her, threatening to shut off her breath. This sicissor-legged sun-browned man in the cheap ill-fitting gray suit . . . this top-heavy rock-steady stranger with the blue-silver eyes . . . this . . . this ex-convict . . . this *father?*

She pulled air into her lungs.

She looked at Uncle George. But he was staring at Mason Campbell. Out of the corner of her eye she saw Deputy Sheriff Bert Bradley pushing his officious way through the crowd. Bradley was a big man, too. Thick-bodied in his black and gray uniform, with a brutal arrogant swing to his shoulders.

"Be of any help to you?" he asked Mason Campbell.

"No, thanks." Her father's voice was flatly resonant— a tone like a saw biting into an empty wooden box.

Bradley frowned. "Guess there ain't no use pretending I'm the welcome wagon." He showed his stumpy teeth. "You know me and I know you; and all these folks here" —he looked over his shoulder at the crowd—"well, they didn't just come down to see the train pull in. They know you, too, and where you been and why. Now this way we start off with all our cards on the table, and it's up to you whether we have a nice friendly game or not."

Mason Campbell nodded, his face expressionless.

"We're willing to live and let live around here, Campbell," Bradley went on in a falsely hearty, bragging voice. "Just because a man's done time is no reason he can't straighten up and make something out of himself."

Stop it! Ming cried silently. What are you trying to do!

"Much obliged to you for explaining it to me," Mason Campbell said dryly, looking past the deputy, over the heads of the crowd, as though trying to locate something or somebody.

"Well, now!" Bradley's voice got heartier with every word. "I see George Peabody and your little gal came in to give you a ride home, but you sure can't pack all this junk in George's car."

Campbell's head moved sharply. His eyes jumped from face to face. For the first time he looked unsure of himself.

Ming stepped forward. She hadn't known what she would do or how she would meet him, but now she simply walked up to him and said, "Hello. I'm Ming."

Mason Campbell's hard mouth stretched in a strange grimace. Then the grimace became a smile and the narrow eyes were full of silver-blue light as he put out his hand and said, "Hello. Hello, Ming."

His hand was dry and warm. Not like Uncle George's hand. She looked up at him. She didn't want to cry.

Then Uncle George came bustling up, and Mason Campbell shook hands with him and there was quite a bit of talk from George and Bert Bradley, and Ming stood beside her father and suddenly it didn't matter if there were a hundred people all around, staring at them. It didn't matter that Bert Bradley was an officious loud-mouthed fool and Uncle George an ingratiating hypocritical loud-mouthed fool.

She looked up at her father. And he looked down at her. He was very grave, not smiling now, but not cold, not hard. He was standing easy, waiting. It gave her confidence somehow. Most people couldn't stand easy, and wait.

"Whatcha got here anyway?" Bert Bradley nudged one of the cardboard boxes with his toe, perhaps harder than he intended. The box skittered across the concrete platform to Ming's feet.

Her father swung his gaze to the deputy, cautiously, almost delicately, as though not to upset some invisible and precarious balance.

"Don't do that." His voice was no louder than before, but it wasn't the same voice.

"Huh?"

"Don't kick those boxes around."

"You're telling *me* to don't *do* something?" Bradley spoke with exaggerated emphasis. He stuck his thumbs in the black cartridge belt he wore slanted across his hips. "I'm a deputy sheriff of this county, Campbell, in case you hadn't noticed. And it just so happens I got good and sufficient reason to ask what you got in them boxes. Now are you gonna tell me, or am I gonna have to find out some other way?"

"Some other way," Campbell said. And then he laughed. It was very surprising to hear him laugh—because Bert Bradley wasn't laughing and nobody else was laughing and there really wasn't anything to laugh about, Ming thought.

"Look, Bert. Let's quit playing Wild West. You're a deputy sheriff sure enough, and I'll give you all due respect. But when you start talking tough, all I can see is the way you looked that day I caught you stealing muskrats off my trap line. You remember that day, don't you, Bert?"

Somebody in the crowd snorted.

"You're starting off real bad," Bradley said. "Real bad. I oughta run you in right now for obstructing a peace officer in his duty."

"Why don't you do that." Campbell's voice was a whisper, deadly as the hiss of a blade coming out of its sheath.

Ming felt her heart leap into her throat. He had shifted so fast!

The crowd of townspeople had been enjoying the byplay, but now they were frozen, not even breathing. In the uncanny stillness Ming heard a rustle and a frightened *peep-peep* from the box at her feet.

Why, that's a baby chicken! she thought in absolute amazement. It was as incomprehensible as hearing a dog bark from inside Aunt Sara's refrigerator.

What was her father doing with baby chickens? Unless he had *stolen* them! Maybe that's why he was so mad!

Bradley stared at Campbell in silence, opening and closing his mouth like a beached shark. But he made no further move.

Mason Campbell turned to Ming. "Where can I hire a truck to cart this stuff out to the farm?"

"Gosh, I don't know."

"I got a little ton-and-a-half pickup, Mase," an old man said from the edge of the crowd. "Parked right out front of the station.

"Don't know me, do you?" The old man stuck out his hand. "Tom Morse. Used to drink your daddy's elderberry wine when you wa'n't kneehigh to a doodlebug."

"Sure! Sure!" Mason grinned.

And it was the same grin! For an instant he was the man in the picture—the boy.

"Can I come with you?"

"Sure," her father said. But old Tom Morse shook his head. "Front seat's all busted. Ain't hardly room for two."

So she had to ride home with Uncle George, and she hated it. She knew she was being silly, but she just didn't want to let her father out of her sight for a minute.

Uncle George was surly. Ming was so full of new enthusiasm that she didn't notice until he rudely interrupted her while she was telling him for the tenth time how wonderful her father looked.

"He's going to find out we ain't all Bert Bradleys," George said. "I'd like to see him push Sam Dunbar around like that."

"Bert Bradley *started* it. I'll bet Sheriff Sam and my father will get along just fine."

George looked at her sourly. "Even the little girl rats don't waste any time getting off the sinking ship, do they?"

Ming felt a flash of sympathy. If Bert Bradley couldn't stand up to Mason Campbell, what chance would Uncle George have?

26

"He's buying himself a load of trouble," George muttered. "You mark my words."

And then George remembered he had to see a man about a piece of property, and wasted more time by parking an unnecessary two blocks away from the Lakeview Inn. As if he were fooling somebody! Ming thought scornfully.

When they finally reached the farm, they found Sara in a tizzy.

"Why, he wouldn't hardly speak to me," Sara said. "Fix me an Alka-Seltzer, will you, honey?"

Ming hurriedly shook a tablet into a glass and filled it with water. "Where is he? Where did he put the chicks?"

"Better make it two. Chicks? What chicks?"

"In the boxes. They're full of baby chicks."

"Baby *chicks!*" George guffawed. "Well, I knew he was a nut, but he oughta know the poultry business is all shot to hell and gone around these parts." George had gained a deal of confidence in the past hour.

"Where *is* he, Aunt Sara?"

"Out in the barn, I guess. He took all those boxes in the barn. Wouldn't come in the house at all. Wouldn't hardly say hello. I had coffee ready and nice chocolate cake . . ."

Ming was halfway to the barn by then. It was a big barn, twice the size of the house, and at one time had been a real working barn. But since her grandfather's death it had held only the Jersey cow, Prissy, for a few years, till Uncle George sold her to meet the payments on his

27

Pontiac. Now there was just the car, and it was only in the barn occasionally, when the weather was bad.

The big doors were standing wide open on their trolleys. Ming hesitated at the threshold. She saw a jumble of empty boxes, but the interior of the barn was dark after the bright sunlight and she couldn't see . . .

"Come on in!"

She saw him then, at the far end, near the old box stalls.

"I thought I could set up in here without too much trouble," he said as she picked her way across the worn and splintered plank floor. "But I guess I was thinking of the barn the way it used to be."

"Why don't you put them in the brooder house," Ming said helpfully. "We only keep a few hens now for eggs, and the brooder house is empty. Course it's probably pretty dirty, too," she added.

"No, no. You never put birds like these where you've kept chickens."

"Birds like what?" The light from the open stall window cut golden through the dust motes, but all Ming could see was a stack of cages. "I thought they *were* chickens."

"You did, eh! Come here."

Ming walked around the stall partition. And stopped short, staring. She couldn't believe it. She absolutely positively could not believe her eyes.

The cages were full of birds. Red birds and pink birds and russet birds, bright birds and dark birds and beautiful clear flaming birds that took her breath away—all hopping back and forth, chirping, cocking their sleek heads in wonder at their new surroundings.

"What do you think of 'em?" Mason asked, almost shyly.

"Why . . . why, they're *canaries!*"

She turned to look at him, unable to overcome her astonishment. He had taken off his coat and tie, and rolled up his sleeves. His white shirt, open half down the front, was smudged and sweat-soaked. She noticed his arms and chest were deeply tanned, and it seemed strange, for a man fresh out of prison.

She looked again at the stack of cages, and saw that this was only the smallest part of them. There were cages on the floor and on the shelf along the other wall, and right at her feet was a large open box full of flat sections which Mason had been assembling into *more* cages.

"Soon as I build me some decent flights," he said, "I'll just use the cages for breeding and training."

"But you didn't have them in *prison* with you, did you?"

"Sure I had 'em in prison with me. I'll tell you about it someday, but right now I gotta get 'em fed and watered and set up for the night." He bent once more to his task, assembling the rest of the cages.

Ming looked down at the top of his head, at the black hair thick and curly, the shoulders, the muscles bunching under the strained shirt. He squatted on his heels, knees up around his ears, light and limber as a boy.

"Can I help? I mean I don't know anything about canaries, but you could show me."

Mason looked up at her. And there was the grin again. For her this time!

29

"Sure. Get me two buckets of water—one hot, one cold. And a clean dipper."

He showed her how to detach the water cups, and rinse and refill them. "We call 'em drinkers. That's your first lesson in bird talk."

He was taking sacks of feed out of another box. She asked him why there were so many different kinds of seeds.

"Probably because we don't really know what a canary needs," he said, grinning. "So we shoot a shotgun full of seeds at them. But the young birds do need a mash to grow on, and plenty of oily seeds like this niger and poppy while they're molting. And I feed the hens a little different than the males—hen with a layer of fat on her makes the best breeder, but you want your males in fighting trim all the time."

He studied Ming for a moment. "You really interested, or just being polite to the old man?"

"Oh, I *am* interested! But I don't know *anything* about birds." She hesitated. "And you're not an old man."

"What I meant was I don't want you to . . . well, to act any different than you ever did. We'll just let this thing go along natural for a while and maybe I'll start feeling as though I actually *am* your old man. Do you understand what I mean, Ming?"

"I guess so. But you know . . . there's one thing . . ." She glanced at him and looked away when he met her gaze. "Well, it's . . . I don't know what to *call* you."

Mase stopped in midmotion, his hand halfway inside a canary cage. He swallowed. "It doesn't matter. You can call me Mase if it's easier for you."

"Well . . ." She didn't want to call him Mase. But she didn't think she could call him Dad. Not right now. And Father just wasn't her style.

"Or you can call me Mr. Campbell, if you want to be formal," Mase said, grinning. "Or . . ." He spread his hands helplessly. "Well, I mean you can call me Dad or Pa . . . or anything you want. It doesn't matter."

It matters to me, Ming thought.

"I could call you Papa."

Mase blinked. He rubbed his chin with his thumb, and a streak of brown and orange flashed out of the cage door he had left open.

"Oh!" Ming was panic-stricken. "He'll get away!"

The canary flew directly to the open window and lighted on the sill, peering out into the wide world.

"Whseeet!" Mase whistled softly through his teeth.

The bird turned its head.

Mase held out his hand. And the bird spread it wings and flew to his outstretched finger.

"Why—my gosh!"

The bird regarded her with a bright skeptical eye. Then suddenly swelled its throat and began to purr— at least that's what it sounded like to Ming. The purr grew louder and became a lovely throbbing note that held Ming spellbound.

"Thinks he's hollow-rolling," Mase said tolerantly. "Didn't have room to keep Rollers down there, but we'll get some now—and then you'll hear some real singing."

"Why he's a *beautiful* singer!"

The bird, as if in appreciation, pointed its beak at the ceiling and hung its full song, like a curtain of crystals, in the quiet air. The afternoon sun, slanting through the

31

window, outlined the canary in golden fire. The canary was so delicate, so beautiful, and so confident . . . the canary should be afraid, Ming thought. Afraid of that strong calloused finger, and of the big heavy-shouldered man with the icy blue-silver eyes and the hard mouth.

The canary finished its song with a self-satisfied flourish and hopped from Mase's finger to his wrist, where it began tugging energetically at the wiry black hairs.

And the man's eyes weren't icy at all, Ming saw. The mouth wasn't hard. The man's face was gentle and bemused. The bird tugged at a hair and looked boldly into the man's face, and the man grinned and with a deft movement transferred the bird back to its cage.

"Canaries," Uncle George said at supper, after Mason Campbell and Ming had finally responded to Sara's repeated calls, "are a little out of my line. You fixing to raise canaries for a living, or is it more like a hobby with you?" George was still floating comfortably on his Lakeview Inn confidence.

"Depends," Mase said. He smiled at Sara. "I've been waiting fifteen years to get my teeth into some real home cooking again, Sara. And this fried chicken was worth the wait."

"Pshaw!" Sara blushed and ducked her head.

Wow and wow! Ming thought. My pappy's a swinger with the ladies as well as with the birds!

"How many birds you got out there anyway?" George was ever so slightly patronizing.

"Three hundred and twelve."

"Three hundred and twelve?"

Mase silently demolished a chicken leg.

"How in tarnation could you keep all them birds ı prison cell?"

"Didn't exactly keep 'em in a cell."

"No? Well, I might be wrong about this, but you *have* been in a penitentiary—or haven't you?"

Mase put down the chicken bone. "That's too stupid to be a question, George. So it must be something else."

"No need to get huffy." George's lardy face reddened in blotches. "You're gonna have to expect questions like that."

Mase shrugged. He glanced at Ming and Sara. "Even if I wanted to talk about prison, you wouldn't understand what I was saying. Nobody can understand who hasn't been there. And it's just as well."

Sara nodded.

Ming stared at her father, the reality of those past fifteen years suddenly burning inside her. What *had* it been like? Would he ever want to tell *her*? She had accepted him so casually, and now for the first time the realization hit her that for him it couldn't be casual at all. She wished she could see inside him, feel for herself what he must be feeling.

It took her a long time to go to sleep that night. The day had been too much. Her father so coldly savage to Deputy Sheriff Bradley, so short with Uncle George. Her father with the lovely golden bird perched on his finger. . . . Which man was he? How could he be both men?

And would he ever . . . would he ever look at her the way he had looked at that little bird?

CHAPTER THREE

"Where is he?"

"Where's who?" Sara was drinking coffee and listening to a man try to sell her wall-to-wall carpeting over the radio.

"My father," Ming said impatiently.

"You mean old birdbrain?"

"I notice you don't talk like that where *he* can hear you."

"Oh, land sakes, Ming! I was just kidding. But it would make a body wonder if prison didn't do something to his head. A big strong grown man like that playing around with canary birds!"

"He's not playing around!"

"Well, what's he doing then? Taking a mortgage on the farm to buy that old truck, and putting those picture windows in the barn. Why, those birds are living better than we are."

Ming poured milk on her cornflakes.

"Now you know yourself, Ming, he's a fool about those birds. Spending all that money." Sara glanced down at Ming's scuffed loafers. "And you without a decent pair of shoes to wear."

"He'd get me some shoes if I asked him."

Sara spread her hands. "Maybe he would and maybe he wouldn't. But he's your father and you shouldn't have to *ask* him."

Ming frowned. She would never admit it to Aunt Sara, but once or twice lately she'd caught herself entertaining similar thoughts. Not that the shoes were important. And not that she begrudged anything her father spent on his birds. The trouble was that her father didn't seem to realize he *was* her father!

He was polite to her and he answered her questions, some of them anyway, and he let her help with the birds when she volunteered. But he never spoke to her with any real warmth or any real freedom. He never even gave her the dickens for making a mistake, never asked her what she was doing or where she had been. And in all the three busy weeks he had been home he had never kissed her, never hugged her, never so much as put his hand on her shoulder.

"What on earth is he going to do with those canary birds!" It was a subject Aunt Sara could pursue tirelessly from morning to night. She seldom mentioned the birds in Mason's presence, but whenever he left the farm she'd scoot out to the barn and spend an hour gazing in helpless fascination at the comings and goings of the feathered creatures whose sole aim in life was evidently to eat her out of house and home.

35

"They're not just plain canary birds," Ming said. "They're some kind of a special breed—a mutant strain, he said—and they're very valuable."

"Valuable! Valuable to who? I saw canary birds in the five-and-dime last time I went to Columbus, good singers too and all you want at five ninety-five."

Valuable to who? It was a very good question, Ming admitted. Her father's birds were pretty, all right, and probably worth more than five ninety-five. But how much more? And if he was figuring on selling them to people around Blairsville—well, he was in for an awful disappointment. He'd never sell three hundred canaries around here in thirty years.

Was it possible her father was a little . . . well, just a little . . . unrealistic on the subject of canaries? Ming wouldn't admit it to Aunt Sara for a million dollars, but privately she agreed that Mason Campbell had picked a most peculiar way to earn a living.

Unless . . . unless it was all a sham. Uncle George thought it was. Uncle George was sure that Mason was using the birds as a cover-up while he waited for his share of the bank loot. But it was hard to believe. Not about the money, but about it being a sham. He worked too hard getting everything just so. Just a certain amount of light and a certain amount of air. Too much sunlight was bad for their color. Drafts were dangerous. He had put in a pipe so the big cages (flights, he called them) would have constantly running water. Now he was trying to decide what kind of heaters he'd have to install for the winter.

A man who was shamming wouldn't go to that trouble. Wouldn't even know how. And the way he handled the birds. Those big calloused hands could pick a canary off a perch as neatly as Aunt Sara reaching into her cupboard for the baking powder.

A canary weighed about two thirds of an ounce, he had told Ming once. And when it was frightened, its heart beat a thousand times a minute. She must have looked her doubt. So he put the bird in her hand. All aquiver—like a tight-wound feathered spring. And so warm! Its body temperature is about 108 degrees, he told her. And then he showed her how to hold the bird so she could press her ear to its back. She heard a sound like the electric motor in a clock. Is that its heart? Her father nodded. She couldn't believe it. Just a whirrrrr. She had been overcome by the mystery of it.

It was the best time to be with her father—when he was with the birds. He would talk to her then, and though it was only about the birds, it was a lot better than not being talked to at all. When he wasn't with the birds, he was usually away somewhere in the old Ford pickup. Looking for buys in seed and lumber and secondhand heaters, he said. Once he came home with half a ton of pure-white sand.

But what was he really looking for? Where did he go and what did he do? Maybe he had a girl friend somewhere. Well, she couldn't hate him for that. Uncle George, in his leering way, had hinted the same thing to Campbell's face. "After fifteen years," George had said, "I'd think you'd have a lot of catching up to do!"

Mason had nodded dubiously, as though he hadn't given it much thought. Uncle George had thrown his cigar away in disgust, and Mason had spoken to him sharply about throwing lighted cigars around a barnyard. George had sulked, flicking his little eyes at Mason, trying to get up his nerve for an answer.

Mason had turned his back on him.

Her father was too hard, Ming thought. Too strong. He didn't seem to care if he hurt people's feelings. He spoke to George as though George were ten years old and not quite bright. Not that George deserved much better, but still . . . it made Ming somehow ashamed. When the two men faced each other, it was like a lobo wolf meeting a fat pig. The wolf stared, cold and incurious. The pig, uncertain, put its head down, afraid to move forward or backward. Woe to the pig if the wolf was hungry!

He wasn't cold and hard toward her, Ming admitted. He was polite and kind—but there was something . . . something . . . Like a pane of glass between them all the time. Her father would be right there, looking at her, and she would move toward him and—bump!—she'd be right back where she started. He didn't duck or dodge or avoid her; he simply stood still and without moving his hands or his eyes or his lips somehow stopped her from getting too close.

Even when she asked him about the canaries: Had he raised them in prison? How had it started? What did he mean by a mutant strain? He had said "Yes" to the first question, and "It's a long story" to the second, and "I'll tell you all about it someday when we've got more time" to the third. She asked him if he was going to sell them, and he said, "Some of them." She asked him if he was going to raise more canaries next year, and he said "Yes." She said, "I wish I knew more about them so I could be more help," and he looked at her and grinned.

It was funny when she stopped to think about it. Not ha-ha funny, though. She remembered how she had felt when Aunt Sara told her Mason Campbell was coming home. First the absolute astonishment—and then the resentment. And then the fear. Fear of what he'd be like and fear of what the town would say and what Billy Gabriel would say and how Miss Dean would act. And fear, even, that this suddenly materialized father would not like her. But it had all emanated from a center point occupied by Ming Campbell, and the concern had been for herself, and the fear had been of the things her father might do to disrupt the tenor of her life in Blairsville.

Never had she imagined it would turn out like this: her father busy and apparently content with his own interests; Aunt Sara and Uncle George standing around on the edges, unmolested but fearful of ghosts; the townspeople, after the first week or so, only mildly curious about Mason Campbell and his barnful of canaries. And Ming Campbell (this was the funny part) standing around on the edges just like Aunt Sara and Uncle George—she wasn't afraid like they were, or at least not of the same things, but she was just as surely on the outside looking in. And Mason Campbell was solidly in the center without knowing or caring that he was in the center.

But that was all right, too. He belonged in the center. Only Ming wanted to be there with him. Or if she couldn't be with him she wanted him to come out where she was—not all the time but just sometimes. Just once, even—if just once he would come right up to her and say, "Hey! It's me! Your old man. I may be a contrary so-and-so, but I'm your dad and don't you forget it! I may be nuts about canaries or maybe just nuts generally, but I'm your father and even if you're not exactly the daughter I'd have picked out if I had any choice, we're going to make the best of it, you and me, and that's one thing you can count on."

But he would never say anything like that, Ming thought sadly. He treated her as though she were maybe the state senator's daughter here on a short visit.

CHAPTER FOUR

Libby Dean had practically no desire to meet Mason
Campbell. She had been intrigued by the tale of his return to town, his resurrection as it were. And she had
been concerned about the effect it might have on Ming.
But only in the disinterested way that any good teacher
might be concerned for a favorite pupil.

Libby was thirty. She had come to Blairsville four
years ago because she was sick and tired of the heavy-
handed administrative pressure in the big-city school
where she had been teaching. At Blairsville High she
taught Junior and Senior English, presided over study
hall twice a week, coached the drama club, and acted as
counselor-without-portfolio for most of the Blairsville
coeds. During the past two summers she had taught full
time at a summer school in Columbus. She was saving
her money, with the as yet only half-formed notion that
someday she and a few other teachers who also had
saved their money might start a school of their own
which they would run in their own way.

She had had two fairly serious romances before coming to Blairsville. None since. The director of the summer school was trying to convince her it was time for another. The director was thirty-five, unmarried, blandly good-looking. But he was soft, in body and mind, and Libby could not abide him.

There were, in fact, a number of things Libby Dean could not abide. She knew she was an opinionated, intelligent woman with a quick, sarcastic turn of speech. She liked men, but she wouldn't knuckle under to them, not even as part of the old love game. She was pretty, in crisp blond green-eyed fashion, and she had a very nearly spectacular figure. But she was beginning to doubt she would ever marry, and she was trying hard to accept this with a reasonable degree of equanimity.

She had been planning to drive up to Columbus on Saturday morning to see a University Theater production of Marlowe's *Dr. Faustus*. But then, Thursday evening, Ming Campbell had knocked on her door, and Libby had decided—after an hour of listening and watching and probing and guessing—that Ming carried higher priority than *Dr. Faustus*. At least for this weekend.

Ming, it seemed, was afraid that . . . well, that her father (it took her a long time to get it out) . . . that her father might have sort of lost his sense of proportion during all those years in prison. He had brought all these birds home with him, and he apparently thought he could make a living with them. Ming didn't know anything about birds, but . . .

"*I* certainly don't know anything about birds," Libby told her.

"Yes, but you know about other things," Ming said. "If you would just come out and talk to him. . . . Maybe you could say you wanted to buy a bird . . . ?"

"No, I couldn't say I wanted to buy a bird. He might sell me one."

"Well, you could say you're just *interested* in birds."

Libby had an answer for that one, too. But the look on Ming's face stopped her.

"All right. I'll come out," Libby said. "But I'll just be your teacher, and you can take me out to look at the birds, and we'll see what develops from there."

It had been unlike Ming Campbell to come pleading for help. That father of hers must be something else! Libby would rather have corrected a hundred freshman themes than go out to that farm and talk to him, but there was simply no choice. Ming was on her way to becoming an exceptional young lady, despite the handicap of living in close daily proximity to her Aunt Sara and Uncle George. And it would be a tragedy if this nutty ex-convict father knocked her off the rails.

On Saturday, when she steered her shiny little Corvair cautiously into the Campbell's cluttered yard, she found Ming waiting for her.

"This wire and stuff is for his birds," Ming whispered. "He's going to build an outdoor flight for them. So they can come out on nice days."

Libby tucked her yellow blouse securely into her skirt and squared her shoulders.

"Lead on, Ming-a-ling. We'll beard this batty birdman in his own blooming belfry."

Ming frowned.

"That wasn't very clever, and I'm sorry. Now let's go talk to your father."

They found him flat on his back, only his incredibly long legs sticking out from under a low, roughly built bench that now ran across the middle of the barn floor.

"This is my teacher, Miss Dean," Ming announced formally. "I thought I'd show her your birds if it's all right."

Mason Campbell poked his head out, staring up at them in surprise. Then he was on his feet with an effortless agility amazing in a man so tall . . . in a man so . . .

He towered above them.

Libby involuntarily stepped back.

He was wearing Levis and a dirty T-shirt. He was sweating from his labor, and she could smell him. What a brute he was!

He nodded but didn't speak.

She had hesitated too long, but now she put out her hand and he shook it, gingerly. He reminded her of some dark-brooding, inarticulate son of toil from a Thomas Hardy novel.

He stood silently by while Ming, obviously embarrassed, tried to tell Libby something about the birds.

Though Libby had never been inside the barn before, she could see how much work he had done. The section where the birds were kept was immaculate. The rough walls had been whitewashed. A bank of new windows flooded the place with light. The birds were in large wire pens extending from the floor to a height of about eight feet. The floor inside the pens was covered with

44

inches-thick shavings and sawdust. For perches he had installed tree branches, and the birds flitted constantly from twig to twig. The birds themselves were brilliantly beautiful, streaks of color as they swooped from shadow to sunlight, and quite unlike any canaries Libby had ever seen.

"These are the young males," Ming said. "They're molting now, but you can see the color of the new feathers coming in."

She could indeed. Feathers so red they looked like splotches of blood. "I didn't even know there *was* such a thing as a red canary."

"Neither did I! See, these are the old males. Aren't they pretty?"

"What are those dark ones? They look like red chocolate."

"I think they're . . ." Ming hesitated. "Those aren't the dilutes, are they?" She looked at her father.

"No, no." He spoke for the first time. His voice was low, with a little rasp to it, but not unpleasant. Not exactly brutish, Libby thought.

"Most people call 'em mahoganies," he went on. "Technically they're known as red-green."

"Green? Mahogany fits them perfectly, but I can't see anything green about them." So we'll talk about the birds, Libby was thinking. He's certainly not going to talk about anything else!

But it wasn't that simple, either. Mason Campbell didn't rise to the bait. He merely shrugged.

"No, seriously, Mr. Campbell," Libby heard herself saying. "I've always been very fond of canaries and I thought I might buy one from you if you have a good singer for sale. But I'd like to know why you call that bird green when it hasn't got a green feather on its body, as far as I can see." She heard her own voice rambling on, felt Ming's astonishment, saw Campbell's slight frown.

"I don't understand it *either*. But I thought I was just dumb," Ming said breathlessly.

"Well, it's a little complicated." Campbell paused and rubbed the side of his jaw with his thumb as if wondering whether to go on with it. "These birds are all Red Factor canaries—but they've got about a dozen different colors that don't make much sense to anybody who isn't a Red Factor breeder. The names come down from the old yellow and green canaries. This bird is called a redgreen because if it had a yellow ground instead of a red ground, it would be green instead of mahogany."

"That certainly clears *that* up." Libby laughed.

Mason seemed unamused.

These Campbells definitely do not appreciate your brand of humor, Libby told herself. Now play it straight or else pick up your marbles and go home.

"Maybe it would help if I knew what you meant by a Red Factor canary," she said humbly.

"Yeah." Mason stared at her for a moment, his face noncommittal. "The name comes from the nineteen twenties," he said, apparently deciding she was entitled at least to common courtesy. "When the German breeders first crossed the black-hooded Venezuelan red siskin with the domestic yellow canary, they got some nice small copper-colored offspring—nothing exceptional, though,

46

and that seemed to be the end of it because in those days most of your animal breeders believed that any cross-species hybrid was necessarily sterile.

"But there were a couple of bird breeders who maybe hadn't read the books. They went ahead and paired up all their crosses, and it turned out that some of these hybrid males were fertile when bred back to a canary hen. Now that was very big news in the bird world of the twenties—about like if a poultryman today came up with a fertile cross between chickens and geese. Breeders all over the world started putting siskins to their canary hens. They figured that by interbreeding the second- and third-generation crosses they'd soon come up with a red canary."

Libby could think of a lot of things the world needed worse than a red canary, but she held her peace.

"Genetics was a new science in those days, you know," Mason went on. "They thought the genes worked in animals the way they did in Mendel's peas—one gene for height and one for shortness and one for curly hair—everything simple and straightforward. So the canary breeders thought it wouldn't be too hard to isolate the gene that gave the siskin his red color, and once they had it fixed in the canary they could concentrate on building up the bird's size and singing ability and so forth. They didn't call it a gene, though—they called it a factor. The *red* factor. Canaries with siskin blood were called red-factor canaries, and the name stuck."

Mason had warmed to his subject, and his listeners, as he spoke. He even smiled once or twice.

Libby was flabbergasted. She had been expecting a

brute, and a brute he had appeared when he sprang out from under that bench. But the longer he talked, the more he sounded like her old zoology professor.

"But it must have worked," she said. "I mean even if they didn't understand the genetics involved."

"No, it didn't work. They ran into all kinds of trouble. Maybe because the first-cross hens weren't fertile; nobody knows for sure. But they couldn't put the real siskin red into the canary. They've been plugging away at it for forty years now, trying to breed a true red canary, and the best they've come up with is a nice deep red-orange."

"You mean that bird isn't red?" Libby pointed to a dazzling bird clinging to the wire in front of them. "Or do you mean it isn't a canary?"

"I think it's a red canary," Mason said, grinning for the first time.

Was he putting her on? Libby wondered. Not that it mattered a whole lot. She couldn't imagine anyone spending forty years trying to develop a red canary, and she doubted it would be worth much if and when you finally achieved it. But she had come out here because Ming was worried that her father might be a little unrealistic on the subject of canaries. To find out if her father was a screwball would be more accurate, Libby thought. She cudgeled her brain for traces of what she had once known about genetics.

"Is the color carried on the X chromosome?"

Mason lifted an eyebrow. "No. Some of the melanin inhibitors are on the X chromosome. Cinnamon color, for instance, is a sex-linked recessive trait. But as you probably know, Miss Dean, gene mapping, even in the fruit fly, has turned out to be much more complicated than the early investigators ever thought it would."

"How fascinating!" She looked at Ming. The girl was staring openmouthed at her father.

"Well," Libby said briskly. "How much do you charge for a canary like that pink-and-white one, Mr. Campbell?"

Mason hesitated. "I don't want to sound unreasonable," he said. "But these birds are bred for the fancy—for people who exhibit at the bird shows. What you want is a house singer. One of my birds wouldn't be worth to you what you'd have to pay for him."

"Oh? Well, I don't want to sound unreasonable either, Mr. Campbell. But how do you know what he'd be worth to me?"

Mason shrugged. "The pink-and-white one's not for sale. He's one of my breeders. You can have that red frost"—he indicated a bird that looked like a ripe strawberry flecked with snow "—for a hundred and fifty."

"*A hundred and fifty!* Dollars?"

"Or you can have this mahogany for seventy-five. He's just a carrier."

"Carrier," Libby said vaguely. She looked at Ming. Mason Campbell's daughter was showing signs of shock.

Libby peered up at Mason in honest bewilderment, and just for an instant his silver-blue eyes returned her gaze. She felt his eyes reaching down inside her, pushing things aside, searching for and finding a hidden, sensitive . . . She dropped her gaze quickly. And found herself looking at the hard curve of his chest outlined by the

49

sweaty T-shirt. In sudden, uncharacteristic panic she turned away, murmuring to Ming that she really had to run.

Once settled in her car, she gave Ming a bright smile. "I guess I wasn't much help, was I?"

"Oh, you were! He never talked like that before. I didn't realize there was so much . . . you know . . . science to it."

"Yes. Well . . ." Libby hesitated. "I don't pretend to know what he's talking about, Ming. And I don't know if he's being . . . realistic or not, either." Again she hesitated. "It's not really the canaries that are bothering you, is it?"

"No!" Ming's eyes—blue, but not the startling silver-blue of her father's—filled suddenly with tears. "No, I wouldn't care if he had a million canaries and never sold the first one. But he's so . . . so *distant*. Why won't he talk to *me*?"

"I don't know. Except that he spent a great many years locked up in a prison where there weren't any little girls to talk to. Or big girls, either," she added thoughtfully. "Maybe he's a little bit afraid of you, Ming."

"Afraid? Him?" Ming snorted.

"I mean of being rebuffed. People aren't always what they seem, you know."

Ming swallowed. "I don't think he's afraid of being rebuffed. I just don't think he likes me very well."

"I'm sure he likes you," Libby said earnestly. But she knew it wasn't enough. Knew that nothing she could say would ever convince Ming. It was between Ming

50

and that strange man in the barn—and how it would work out, time alone would tell.

"Now you keep me posted," Libby said, pressing the starter. "And don't worry too much, Ming. Any man with the brass to ask a hundred and fifty dollars for a canary has *got* to have something going for him."

No sooner had Libby pulled away than an ancient black rattletrap came shuddering up the driveway and ground to a halt in front of Ming.

She knew the driver. Mrs. Elvira Waterman, a widow, seventy-five if she was a day, who lived alone in a crumbling brick house near the school.

"Hello! Hello!" Lean and spry as an elderly cricket, Elvira Waterman hopped out of the car carrying an empty bird cage.

"Is your daddy to home?"

Ming nodded cautiously.

"Well, don't just stand there like a statue! Where is he? Want to buy a bird from him!"

Ming cringed inwardly. She kind of liked Mrs. Waterman, despite the old lady's acrid tongue.

"I really don't think he wants to sell any, Mrs. Waterman."

"Nonsense!" The old lady waved the empty cage. "My Dickie Bird passed away in his sleep last week. Eight years old and he cheered me up every blessed day of his sweet little life. Now go get your daddy like a good girl."

Ming did as she was told. Mrs. Waterman was due for the shock of *her* sweet little life, but there was no use arguing with her.

Her father surprised Ming, though. He listened with interest to the old lady's account of Dickie Bird's demise and then politely escorted her to the barn.

"Bad time to buy birds," he said. "The molt——"

"I know, I know! That's why I came out here 'stead of going to the pet shop in Columbus. Heard you were a real breeder and figured I could trust you to pick me out a nice healthy youngster who'll keep me company maybe for the rest of my days."

Oh, Lord! The poor old lady! Ming knew what would happen when Mason showed her the price tag. Mrs. Waterman would either faint or else hit him over the head with her bird cage.

"Goodness gracious!" Mrs. Waterman said. "I never dreamed you had such birds as *these,* Mason." She looked up at him, her faded gray eyes sparkling. "You don't mind me calling you Mason, do you? You wouldn't remember, I expect, but I used to come out here when your mother was alive, years and years ago."

"I remember." Mason smiled.

"Well, good, good! But that's neither here nor there. I just had it in mind to get me a yellow canary, Mason. I wouldn't be able to afford any such a bird as these."

Mason rubbed his chin with his thumb. "Well, yeah . . . some of 'em do run a little steep, but I've got a couple of birds here that wouldn't cost you *too* much." He glanced out of the corner of his eye at Ming. She shook her head violently. Mrs. Waterman was staring entranced at the flight of young males, most of whom were diligently practicing for the day they'd be real singers.

"Now I've got an early-hatched bird in there who's practically finished his molt," Mason said, ignoring his daughter's frantic signal. "Starting to warble pretty good, too—that is, if you don't mind chopper song."

Mrs. Waterman peered up at him, a flush of excitement on her soft, papery cheeks.

"That mahogany bird," Mason said. "I do believe he's going to make a pretty fair singer."

And before Ming or the old lady knew what he was up to, he stepped through the walk-in door and captured the canary with one swift swipe of his huge hand.

"Let's just see how he looks in your cage."

The startled canary, finding himself in a completely new world, stood tensely alert on Dickie Bird's perch. If he had been beautiful in the flight, he was twice as beautiful in this small cage, Ming realized. Deep chocolate-red, so sleekly feathered he looked carved from wax, eyes bright as black diamonds.

"Oh, my!" Mrs. Waterman said.

"You oughta feed him boiled carrots for another week or so," Mason said, "to set his color good. And keep him out of drafts for a few days."

Mrs. Waterman shook her head helplessly. "I'd never let him get in a draft, Mason. But I can't . . . how much is he?"

"Well, he's twelve dollars and fifty cents."

"Oh, that's a very fair price, Mason! But I don't have that much with me." The old lady dropped her eyes in embarrassment. "Could I . . . could I give you ten dollars now and the rest next month?"

"Wait a minute," Mason said, bending forward to inspect the canary. "This bird's got a drop tail—won't hurt his singing but cuts his value down."

"Where?" Mrs. Waterman peered at the bird suspiciously. "I don't see anything wrong with his tail."

"You can have this bird for nine dollars if you don't mind the tail," Mason said. "Or I'll pick you out a good twelve-and-a-half-dollar bird, whichever you like."

"Mason! Mason! I know a little something about canaries and I know I couldn't touch this bird for thirty dollars in the pet shop. I'm going to pay you ten dollars now and next month I'll give you the other two fifty."

"Fair enough." Mason grinned. "You better take some of my feed along, so it won't be too big a change for him." He quickly filled two paper sacks with seeds, answering the old lady's questions about the bird's dietary needs.

Not until she was gone did he again meet Ming's eyes.

"That's the very same bird you wanted to charge Miss Dean seventy-five dollars for!"

"No, that was a different——"

"The same bird!"

"Well, maybe it was at that. I can't hardly tell 'em apart."

"Hah! You're borrowing money from the bank and you turn around and practically give away a seventy-five dollar canary."

"Well, she needed a bird," Mason said lamely. "She knows how to take care of a bird."

"Oh, I see. You only sell birds to old ladies who *need* them. At twelve dollars and fifty cents apiece!"

"Now you sound like your mother," Mason said, grinning at her. "She never approved of my financial dealings, either."

"She didn't?" Ming was acutely aware that for the first time since he came home she had spoken right out to him without wondering what he would think.

"I never had much sense with money. Looks like I never will have."

"Was he really worth seventy-five dollars, or were you just teasing Miss Dean?"

"It's hard to say right now what he's worth. Like a farmer who raises a good bull, say. In July it's just another good yearling bull, and he might not get over a few hundred dollars for him. In August he takes the bull to the state fair and wins Grand Champion and all of a sudden the bull is worth twenty thousand dollars. Not only that, but the price on the bull's brothers and sisters goes way up because there's now a demand for this bull's bloodline."

"Are you going to put your canaries in the fair?"

"Not in the fair. In the bird show. The National Cage Bird Exhibition, they call it."

"And if they win they'll be worth a lot of money?"

Mason lifted his shoulders. "They've got to do more than win. They've got to be recognized for what they are."

"For what they *are?* Honest to Pete, if you're not the worst person in the world to *explain* anything!"

"I guess so," Mason said. "But it's a long story, and I just didn't think you'd be interested."

"Of *course* I'm interested. You know what the trouble with you is?"

"What?" He looked slightly alarmed.

"You're too defensive about these darn birds. You don't think anybody will understand why you're raising them, and you don't even *try* to explain it. My gosh, I'm your daughter, you know. I'm interested in whatever you're interested in, but you won't even give me a chance!" She was almost crying.

Mason Campbell frowned. Then he opened his eyes wide and stared at his daughter. "I'll be . . ." he said softly. He upended an empty nail keg. "Sit down and make yourself comfortable." He shook a cigarette out of his pack and lighted it. Then he looked at Ming, frowning as though he had never seen her before. "You smoke? Never thought to ask."

"No." She smiled. "No, I don't smoke." The nail keg was just about the best thing she had ever sat on. She looked at her father and waited for him to begin.

CHAPTER FIVE

"It all started," Mason Campbell said, "back in 'fifty-one. I'd been in prison five years, but every morning I woke up, it was like the first day all over again. I just couldn't get it through my head I was going to have to spend fifteen or twenty years in that place. Down there they work most of the able-bodied men on the chain gang, but they wouldn't put me out. 'Fraid I'd run. So I had to stay at Raiford and I didn't like it.

"Me and the warden had many a go-round. And when I wasn't fighting the warden, I'd like as not be fighting some con. I couldn't get along with anybody, didn't want to get along. What they call a hardnose.

"Five years of it . . . My nose was getting sore from banging against steel and concrete, but I had it in my mind I couldn't back down."

Ming was sitting on the nail keg, elbows on her knees, chin cupped in her hands. She sat absolutely still.

Mason Campbell prowled restlessly back and forth in

57

front of the flights. It was suddenly very important to him that his daughter understand. He didn't want to dwell on those early prison years. The brutal, sordid details would only shock and confuse her.

"Then one day the warden came to see me. I was in an isolation cell, had been there for five months. This warden was an old-timey southern prison official—which means he didn't know anything about sociology or psychology or modern penology, at least not the way they teach it in books. His idea of rehabilitation was a twelve-hour day loading trucks or clearing right-of-way —with lots of sowbelly and beans to keep your strength up. After work you could do pretty much what you liked. Work leathercraft, play poker, sit up and read all night if you wanted to. I'm not saying that's the best way to run a prison, but after you've talked to boys who've done their time in the new-style prison you wonder if it really makes much difference.

"Anyway, this warden let me bang my head on the bars for five years, and then when he thought the time was ripe he walked right into my cell one day, no guard with him, and sat down on my bunk and told me he had a job for me.

"I just stood there looking at him. He was a scrawny wizened-up old cracker, name of Snodgrass, face and neck cut with a million wrinkles from that Florida sun. Had brown bulgy eyes that always made me want to grab his skinny neck and see if I could pop 'em out the rest of the way. But this time I just stood there and listened to him.

"Said he had a job in the pump house, needed a man

58

to live right there, take care of the filters, and so forth. Said it was a lonesome job, no guard, no other cons allowed down there. Wanted to know if I'd like to take a crack at it.

"Well, for a minute I didn't know what to do. Felt almost like bawling. Started to tell him No. Tell him he couldn't bribe me. That was how my mind was working in those days. But it hit me all at once that this man didn't need to bribe me. He could leave me right there in isolation for the next ten years and his prison would go right along just as smooth as if I was dead.

"So I told him sure, I'd like to try it. And he took me out of the cell right then and walked across the yard with me and got me some clean clothes and a decent meal.

"That was the beginning. Something happened to me. I don't know what it was, but all of a sudden I didn't feel any urge to bust every guard in the mouth just because he was a guard. I wasn't exactly happy, mind you. It was still prison, and there were lots of things I wanted to do and couldn't do. But here I was in a room of my own with a job to do and nobody breathing down my back.

"Sure, sometimes I'd get ideas about crashing out, which I probably could have done any night there was a storm. I'd get to thinking about you and the old man. But I knew I'd never be able to come back here—just be on the run till they caught me, or else hiding for the rest of my life."

He stopped and gazed intently at Ming. "And I'll tell

you something else, because I know you must be thinking about it. I thought about my ex-buddy and what I'd do to him when I caught up with him. Sure I did." Mason grinned. "The warden probably thought about it too. He'd drop in once in a while, have a cup of coffee and talk about his dogs. He raised pointers, entered 'em in field trials all over the country. Never once did he mention the stickup or the missing loot or my ex-partner. But I realized later what a chance he was taking. He'd have caught a barrel of hell if I had cut through that triple fence they use at Raiford in place of a wall. Might've cost him his job."

"He must have been a wonderful man," Ming said, breaking her silence.

Mason grinned. "You'd have a tough time convincing most of the Florida cons there's anything wonderful about him. They'll tell you he's hard as a rattail file. Which he is, in some ways. But he's got guts, and he trusts his own judgment. I've seen him make trusties out of men his deputy wanted to keep in leg irons.

"He liked to talk about his dogs, though, and since he was a good storyteller, I didn't mind listening. One day he brought a big ticked pointer female in for me to look at. The dog took to me and didn't want to leave. After they were gone I got to thinking how nice it would be to have a dog for company, so next time Snoddy showed up I asked him if maybe he wouldn't sell me a runt out of his next litter.

"He hemmed and hawed around some but finally said he couldn't do it. Dogs were against the rules inside the walls, and if he let me have one there'd be six hundred other guys wanting one.

" 'Get lonesome down here, do you?' he asked me.

"I told him not exactly lonesome but sometimes in the evening it would be nice to have a dog to talk to. Didn't think anymore about it, but in a day or two here he comes back and he's carrying a kind of awkward-looking package wrapped in brown paper.

" 'This prob'ly sunthin you won't want,' he said, setting his parcel down on a bench and kind of snuffling through his nose and squinting all around the room but not looking at me.

" 'I was telling it at table last night how I had to turn you down on that dog,' Snoddy said, taking out his red bandanna and wiping his neck. 'My daughter spoke up—she's only fourteen and full of fool notions—she spoke up and said she wanted to give you one of her birds if *that* wasn't against the rules. Which I had to tell here there wasn't any rule one way or the other on birds, and in fact I know they's a few in the cellblock.'

"I was standing there trying to make sense out of it. About the last thing in the world I wanted was a bird, but if Snoddy's daughter had sent it in, it was going to be awful hard to refuse.

" 'Now if you don't want it just say so,' Snoddy said, finally getting around to unwrapping the cage. 'If it was me I wouldn't want a dang bird neither, but my daughter raises them, you know, and she just can't understand that some people wouldn't take a dang bird as a gift.

" 'Ain't in the same league with a dog, natchally,' he said, shucking off the last of the paper and setting this old brass bird cage down on my table. 'But then again it beats a cockroach if a fella's lonesome for somebody to talk to.'

61

"It was just a yellow canary," Mason said softly, re-membering. "With a black patch over the right eye. What you call a chopper or a warbler—though at that time of course the only choppers I knew anything about made considerable more noise than a bird.

"The canary didn't do anything. Sat on his stick and gave the room the once-over, calm as you'd expect a warden's daughter's canary to be.

" 'Now you don't have to keep him, Mason,' the warden said. He always called you by your first name even if he was sentencing you to thirty days on bread row. 'It was just a tomfool notion . . .'

"But I told him sure I wanted to keep him, and I could see the old man was sort of pleased no matter how much he kept running the bird down. I told him to thank his daughter for me and he said he would, and there I was, alone with this fool canary."

Mason squatted down on his heels across from Ming, his hard, blocky face curiously relaxed, his eyes full of remembered pleasure. It was the first time he had ever told this story to anyone, perhaps even to himself, and it was all as bright and new in his memory as if it had happened yesterday.

Ming hadn't moved. An invisible weaver was spin-ning a new thread between her and her father. Fine as gossamer at first, growing stronger now. And she wouldn't move. Couldn't move.

"I walked around kind of careful so as not to scare the bird," Mason said, smiling. "He was so damned little and fragile and he kept that beady black eye on me every minute. The warden had left me a box of seeds, and I figured I better feed him before I went to bed in case he woke hungry in the night. All this time, mind you, the bird hadn't let out a peep. So I reached inside his cage real slow, and just as I touched his seed cup that bird let out a squawk and tore into my hand like a gamecock attacking an elephant. Startled me so, I spilled his seeds all over the room.

"He stood there on his stick, squawking, hackles up, flapping his wings, daring me to try it again. I didn't know what to do. Thought maybe he was having a fit. Sat down and rolled myself a cigarette, and soon as the bird saw I was whipped he started to sing—just pouring it out, like he was never going to get another chance.

"Well, I don't suppose I'd ever heard a canary sing before. I mean—to be in a room alone with one and really listen to him. Didn't know what I was hearing—but this bird had a special note that I found out later is called bell, and he really rang it that night."

Mason lifted his hand. "Hear that?" he asked Ming, jerking his thumb at one of the flights. "That's a fair bell right there."

She heard a hundred canaries singing, and had no idea which one her father meant. But she smiled and nodded.

"That bird was hand-raised, I found out later, and tame as a cocker spaniel. He didn't like anybody poking their hands in his house, but when I let him out he'd sit on my shoulder, and when I ate I had to watch him or he'd be right down in the plate. I'd never seen a bird like that before, and after I'd had him a week I wouldn't have taken a hundred dollars for him.

"Then one day about a month later, middle of April it was and springtime even in prison, here comes the warden with another bird, tucked inside his shirt this time. Said his daughter thought my bird might be getting lonesome, so she was sending in a little lady bird to keep him company. Straight-faced as a judge, he was—like he didn't have any idea what he was letting me in for.

"The hen was a dainty little thing, cinnamon-variegated, and my old Bully bird went for her like a hog goes for slops. I let 'em both fly around as they pleased, since there wasn't anybody in the pump house but me and I didn't mind what little mess they made. Wasn't two weeks later till the hen was pulling threads out of my blanket and building herself a nest in a coffee can half full of washers I kept up on a shelf. I never paid a whole lot of attention as I was busy right then repacking the pumps. I did notice she was sitting on the nest all the time and I tried to get a look inside, but she wouldn't move and Bully raised so much hell I decided to leave 'em alone.

"One morning I was drinking my coffee and Bully came down for some crumbs like he always did. But this time he offered me something in return. Half an eggshell. Laid it right down beside my cup.

"Well, I felt almost the way I guess I would have felt if I'd been around the day you were born." Mase grinned at his daughter. "Mind you. Big old hulk like me, born and brought up on a farm—but when those two damn little birds hatched that egg in the coffee can it was like something brand new happening for the first time in the world.

"Two days later they had four young ones, and Bully and the hen were on the hop from dawn till dark trying to fill those gaping mouths. About the seventh day the chicks' eyes opened up and they were feathering out a little and starting to look like birds. I was sending panic calls through the warden to his daughter, finding out how to feed 'em and so forth. And the warden was down every day to see how my family was getting along.

"From then on things just sort of got out of control. Bully and the cinnamon hen raised fourteen young that season, and when those birds went into the molt my room looked like somebody had opened a feather pillow and shook it loose. Had to get me some fine wire screen and make a big cage. Warden let me go, thinking probably it was a passing thing and next year I'd lose interest.

"The next year I bred old Bully back to six of his daughters, and before the warden knew what was happening I had fifty-seven canaries and you could hear those birds singing clear up to the ball diamond.

"Old Snoddy was sort of torn between two emotions. He had started it, you see, and he was kind of proud in a way that I was having such good luck with them. But he was a little worried, too, about what would happen if one of the commissioners wandered into the pump house someday and got attacked by forty or fifty canaries.

"And I had another problem—didn't have the money to buy proper seed, so I asked Snoddy if I could make a deal with one of the pet stores in Jacksonville, trade off half my birds for a supply of feed and some cages. I'd been making cages out of wire screen, and that pump house looked worse than Tobacco Road.

"Snoddy thought that sounded like a good idea. Cut

down the bird population and neaten up the premises at the same time. Even brought me the address of a reliable bird dealer from his daughter.

"It was a funny thing, but every time Snoddy got into the act the bird situation went the direct opposite from what he had in mind. This dealer in Jacksonville was an old man in his seventies, been breeding and selling birds all his life. Wrote me a real nice letter and told me to leave my surplus birds with the guard at the gate on such and such a day and he'd drive out from Jacksonville himself to pick them up. Then the next day he'd bring me out the seed and cages and a statement of what credit I had coming, if any, depending on whether the birds were any good.

"Snoddy thought that was a slipshod way to do business but agreed I didn't have a lot of choice. So I did it, and when the guard called me the next day to come pick up my stuff, I found I needed a truck to cart it back to the pump house. That old man had given me a hundred and fifty dollars' worth of credit for thirty mixed birds, way more than they were worth, I found out later. I had a couple hundred pounds of seed and a dozen double-breeder cages and a case of cuttlebone and other stuff I didn't even know what it was for. He had also sent along a stack of old bird magazines and some books, including *Stroud's Digest,* and soon's I glanced in those books I caught a glimmer of how much I didn't know about canaries.

"But the biggest thing he sent, so far as getting me hooked on birds for once and all, was a breeding pair of Red Factors. Told me I could send 'em back if I didn't want 'em. But told me that's where the money was if I wanted to raise canaries for profit.

"They were just average orange birds, but at that time I'd never seen anything but my green and yellow choppers, so I set that pair up in a shady spot and spent the rest of the day admiring them.

"Next thing, I started reading through all the magazines cover to cover and studying Stroud's book. Didn't go to bed at all that night. Next day I cleaned out all my old wire screen and built some shelving for the new cages. In a week I had the place looking halfway decent, birds all down on one wall with a curtain I could pull across to cover them in case we ever did get an inspection from some nosy commissioner.

"Up till then, you see, the birds had just been a kind of plaything, and I had never looked ahead one day to the other. But when I got to reading those bird books I began to understand that with time and care I could build me up a stud of birds right there in the pump house that would be just as good as any birds in the world. All I had to do was get me a few pairs of good sound stock to start with and then pay attention to how I paired up the offspring.

"Found out later it wasn't quite that simple, but the basic idea was right. And it gave me a whole new outlook on life, Ming. Up till then I'd just been putting in my time, with a sort of vague hope that once I got out of prison everything would somehow take care of itself. But now I sat down and took a look at myself. I was twenty-eight years old and didn't have any more idea of how to earn a living than when I was eighteen.

And I had to admit I wasn't particularly interested in learning a trade and working the rest of my life for wages. Didn't have the schooling or the head for any of the professions. Couldn't see myself as a businessman, wasn't too fond of farming—and damn sure couldn't go back in the Army.

"But now I had stumbled onto something that I liked, something I just naturally wanted to do. I didn't stop to think if I was being practical or anything like that. All I knew was that these birds had caught my abiding interest, and I made up my mind right then that I was going to spend the rest of my life with them.

"I didn't tell Snoddy, though. Didn't want to get him alarmed. What I did first was search through the bird magazines for the people who were the big winners at the shows. Then I'd write to 'em and see what they wanted for a pair of their best birds. Prices for winners were awful high, and I got a little discouraged till I hit this fella out in California who wrote back and said he thought anybody who wanted birds bad as I did ought to have them. Said he was sending me some of his best stock and I could pay him whatever I could afford.

"What do you think of that?" Mase asked his daughter, the wonder of it still with him. "Man three thousand miles away sent me four good birds just because he thought I ought to have them. Name was Sampson Remarque. And before we got done I suppose I wrote him fifty letters over a period of years, always asking a million questions, and he answered every one.

"So the next spring I had these two pairs of his and they were beauties. And the pair from the dealer in

Jacksonville. Plus about twenty of my choppers. What I did was breed as many young as I could from the choppers and sold 'em to the old man in Jacksonville. Also sold a few young Red Factors but kept the best ones for my next year's breeding stock. By the time I paid Remarque a fair price for what he had sent me and stocked up with seed and supplies I didn't have any cash left over, but I had fifteen good Red Factor hens and ten nice males, and when Snoddy came around he was pleased to see I was down to twenty-five birds.

"At the end of the next breeding season I had a hundred thirty-five canaries in the pump house and Snoddy almost had a batch of kittens when he found out what I was up to. Said he wasn't running no commercial bird-breeding farm. Said it was strictly illegal for convicts to compete with organized business in the open market. Said he didn't mind me trading off a few birds to meet expenses, but if the commissioners ever found out I was wholesaling canaries for a cash profit there'd be hell to pay and no pitch hot.

"Well, there went my scheme for building a bankroll. Snoddy finally did let me sell a hundred birds that year, and even at wholesale prices they brought me close to a thousand dollars. But he said no more cash transactions. It took the starch out of me for a week or so. Even considered giving up the whole project. But then I'd get to looking at the birds I had left—naturally, I'd saved the cream of the crop—and I decided to go along on a small scale. Breed a few of my best birds each year and concentrate on improving the strain.

"I was starting to study genetics by then, getting books

69

from the state library, and the more I learned, the more I realized how ignorant I was. Pretty soon I was getting into nutrition, finding out about amino acids and vitamins and the rest of it. And then I had to take a few courses in algebra and chemistry in order to understand the books I wanted to read—so in the end it turned out for the best when Snoddy put the damper on my big breeding program. Otherwise I'd have probably been so busy trying to make money I never would have taken the time to learn about the birds themselves.

"Trouble is, canaries have never been researched the way poultry has, for instance. Not enough money in small cage birds to finance it. So you can't find any real scientific information on proper diet or housing or breeding or anything else. But I was going along, trying to see how much poultry science could be applied to canaries—and that's when it happened, six years ago this past spring.

"A dimorphic hen hatched out a chick that looked different even in its baby feathers. Father was a good dilute variegated red cinnamon, and all I was trying for in that pairing was better feather texture. But this one smoky-looking chick stood out from its nestmates. Couldn't figure what it was till I blew up his feathers and saw the dark underflue—clear bird with a dark underflue, it was supposed to be impossible.

"I don't even know what an underflue *is*," Ming interrupted, apologetically.

Instead of answering, Mase stepped quickly into the hen flight and returned holding two birds. "See the difference in color?"

"Well, one is red and the other is more orange."

Turning them belly up, he blew gently into the feathers. "See? The red color is only in the outer tip of the feather, though it looks solid when the feathers are lying flat. The underflue is that downy part of the feather next to the body. On the orange bird it's white, on the red bird it's slaty-gray. Now, on a cinnamon or mahogany canary that underflue is always gray or black, but on clear birds—those without any visible dark markings—that underflue was always white, and so far as I know it's white on every clear canary in the world except the ones in this barn."

"And that's what makes them so much redder?"

"I'm not sure it *makes* 'em redder, but it's tied in with the redness somehow. Sampson Remarque thinks I've got a double dilute. I've never shipped one of these birds out, but most of the breeders in the country have heard about them by now—course they don't believe I've really got the red canary," he added. "And I can't blame them. Too many people have claimed it over the years, and then their bird turned out to be color-fed or maybe a freak that wouldn't reproduce itself."

"But why is it so important to have a red canary? I guess that's the thing I really don't understand."

"It's not important," Mase said, grinning. "Same way lots of things are not important—unless you happen to want them and then they become very important. To me personally a white marigold isn't important at all, but one of the big seed companies has a standing offer of ten thousand dollars to the first plant breeder who comes up with a pure white marigold. So the white marigold is important to a lot of people, same as the red canary is to a lot of other people. Or the football championship, or a new system of bidding in bridge, or the latest fashions in women's clothes—it might be hard to prove that any of these are important in themselves, but they become important if they interest us, and I'm willing to let it go at that."

"Me too." Ming smiled happily. "And you mean all your birds came from that one little baby?"

"Yep. I didn't know what I had till the chick molted, and then when I saw the color, I was almost afraid to believe it. So next season I bred him to every hen he'd take. And you know what?"

Ming shook her head.

"He didn't throw a single bird with dark underflue. Knew he wasn't a dilute then. It'd have shown up in the young hens. Mated him back to his daughters the next year, on the off chance I might have caught me a mutant recessive. And that's what he was. Gave me ten clear young with dark underflue that year, out of twenty-five chicks hatched. Every bird in this barn is descended from him."

Mase stood up and put the two hens back in the flight. Over his shoulder he said, "Guess I got a little wound up, yammering on about these birds. You probably got a hundred things you'd rather be doing."

"No, I haven't," she said with great seriousness. "I'm just sorry I'm so stupid I can't understand half of it."

"You're a long way from stupid, honey."

She looked up at him, on a caught breath, her eyes instantly full of tears.

72

"What's the matter?" Mase was close to panic. This slim beautiful girl had awed him at first glance. He had expected her to be pretty and round-eyed like her mother. But Ming, though still leggy and gracefully awkward, already had her mother beat forty ways for looks. And it wasn't just the looks. Ming was as shy and sweetly tremulous as a wild fawn.

"You . . ." She looked at the scuffed toe of her moccasin. "You never called me honey before. Just plain Ming."

"Oh." He dropped to his heels in front of her and put his big calloused finger under her chin and lifted her head. "And you never call me anything. I guess you know that, don't you?"

"I know," she said in a small voice.

"Well, it takes time to get acquainted," he said easily, surprising himself with his calmness. "Father's just a word. So's daughter. Be a mistake to think you're supposed to have ready-made feeling for some stranger just because he's got the word Father tacked onto him."

She shot him a quick, cautious glance. "I suppose so. Just like a father wouldn't have any . . . any feeling for his daughter. I mean if he never saw her till she was fifteen."

Mase bit hard on his own teeth. He could feel his jaw crack. "Oh, I wouldn't say that necessarily. Can't speak for other fellas, but now you take me for instance . . ." He paused and cleared his throat.

Ming waited. Not breathing. Not looking at him now.

"What I'm trying to get at," Mase said, driving the

words painfully through his lips, "is I know I've been a lousy father and I wouldn't expect you to welcome me with open arms. But I'm going to try to make it up best I can."

Ming raised her eyes. "You don't have to make anything up. Not to *me*. Just as long as . . . I mean . . ." Her voice trembled. "If you *like* me. If you want me for your daughter. That's all I care about."

Mase was stricken dumb.

"Do you?"

"Hell yes!" he said gruffly. "Don't mean to swear so much. Lived alone too long, I guess."

"You can swear all you want. Don't worry about things like that. They're not important."

He grinned fondly at her. "No, they're not important. But you're important, Ming. Most important thing in the world to me, and I want you to remember that in case I don't get around to saying it very often."

She smiled at him. Smiled, and her eyes filled with tears, and suddenly she threw her arms around his neck and was crying her heart out on his shoulder.

He let her cry for a while. Then he took out his handkerchief and held it so she could blow her nose.

"Nobody ever helped me blow my nose before!"

"Maybe that's one of the things dads are good for."

"Yes." For a moment he was afraid she was going to start all over again. But she shook her head fiercely and wiped the tears away and then sighed a tremendous long sigh. "I feel better."

"So do I. Feel like I just came home, by God!"

74

CHAPTER SIX

The secretary's practiced eye caught the storm warnings as soon as her boss walked into the office. Fred Sander had his days, and this, Muriel knew, was going to be one of them. She had been his secretary for three years now. And though the pay was good, and the work was not too hard, she often wondered why she stuck.

Fred Sander was a royal pain in the neck to work for, and you couldn't get around it. But he had this other side, too. He could be charming when he wanted to be. Charming and appealing and infinitely persuasive.

He was a man who favored Italian silk suits and pale ties. He had a mobile, expressive face marred by great sagging pouches under his liquid brown eyes. He had gone bald in a peculiar fashion that affected only the front half of his head. It made his forehead seem a foot high, and with the weary pouched eyes gave him a certain air of decadent elegance. But why settle for decadent elegance, Muriel often wondered, when a hairpiece and twenty minutes of cosmetic surgery could give you back fifteen years?

Fred Sander would have agreed with her—in principle, that is. He had been torn between vanity and prudence for a long time now, ever since the hair started to go. In the end it might not make any difference. At best it might make a difference of two or three seconds. But the inescapable thing was that a difference of two or three seconds might also be the difference between life and death.

When Mason Campbell came looking for him. And he would come—Fred Sander had no doubt of that. And he would come with a gun in his hand. And if the pouches and the bald head delayed positive recognition for even two seconds, it might give Fred Sander the edge he needed. Because he would recognize Mason Campbell—across a thousand years and a million miles—instantly. Those eyes—like quicksilver reflecting a blue sky—and the walk—that loose-swinging walk—and the look of the man—all shoulders and legs. Fred Sander would recognize him on sight, at any angle, any distance. And when he saw him he would have to kill him without any hesitation whatever.

It was that simple. There was no alternative. The police, and the chances of getting caught, and what would happen when they found out who the dead man was—all these things were beside the point. Because if he didn't kill Mason Campbell, why then Mason Campbell would kill him. Of all things in heaven and earth that was the one thing Fred Sander was most sure of.

The safe thing and the smart thing would be to take

the offensive. Fred Sander had realized that years ago. During the middle years he had comforted himself with the half-formed plan of how, a month or so before Campbell was due out, he would hire a professional killer to do the job for him. Meet Campbell practically at the prison gate and blow him away before he ever got out of first gear. It had all seemed so easy, planning it that way. But then, in the twelfth year, it had slowly and painfully dawned on Sander that he didn't know when Campbell would be released. In the beginning he had thought that twenty years meant twenty years, but it had gradually sifted through to him, from reading and TV, that twenty years could mean almost anything.

He couldn't find out what it meant in Campbell's case, not without asking someone to find out for him, and Fred Sander had never mentioned Mason Campbell's name to a living soul and had no intention of doing so now.

That's when it occurred to him that hiring the gunman would not be the simple thing he had thought it would be. Item: He would have to kill the gunman as soon as Campbell was dead, or else risk paying perpetual blackmail and living in constant fear. Item: He didn't know any gunmen, and didn't know any people who had ever admitted to him that they knew a gunman.

In the beginning, when he had been running and hiding, he had promised himself—and in good faith, at the time—that if Campbell stood tight and if the day came that the running and hiding was over, why then he would do everything in his power to make it right with Mason Campbell. He dreamed of smuggling money into the prison, to make Campbell's time as easy as possible. Or helping him escape if that's what he wanted. He dreamed of investing the bank money and holding it in sacred trust, and then when Campbell's twenty years were up he would meet him at the gate and hand him a bankbook with deposits of, say, a hundred thousand dollars, all free and clear in Mason Campbell's name.

Dreams like these made Fred Sander feel good. Sometimes he'd actually get choked up thinking about the wonderful things he would do for Mason Campbell, and thinking about the wonderful thing Mason Campbell was doing for him.

One thing he didn't think about too often was the hellish moment the police guns had opened up, Campbell crying out once, then falling, the Thompson clattering into the gutter. They had been only a few feet from the car. He could have stopped. Yes, he could have stopped. Maybe even grabbed the Thompson and sent the cops ducking for cover with a burst or two. When he did think about it he saw the whole thing in his mind's eye. He was holding the tommy gun in one hand, dragging Campbell with the other. Into the car. Campbell, okay except for his leg, firing through the rear window as they roared away to safety. It was a pretty fantasy. But Fred Sander knew it would never have turned out that way. The instant he stopped, he'd have been knocked down by police bullets. And besides, there had been absolutely no possible chance of his stopping. He had been running for his life, out of his mind with terror. And it had been a miracle that he got away.

Campbell would understand that.

Of course he understands, Fred Sander kept telling himself. Otherwise he'd have ratted on me. He knows the money's safe, and he knows I'll take care of him.

But he hadn't taken care of him, and it was too late now to make amends even if he wanted to. Which he didn't.

Back in '47 when Fred Sander finally stopped running from shadows he took what was left of the bank loot, something over fifty thousand dollars, and invested it in real estate. Fred Sander was no fool. He knew he could never again try anything like that bank robbery. So it was a question of using what he had and making it do for the rest of his life.

In 1947 the field, any field, was wide open for the man with guts and vision and a bankroll. Fred Sander bought an old mansion on Chicago's near North Side, cut it up into wallboard apartments, filled it with tenants, and sold it at 110 percent profit.

Now, fourteen years later, he was president and sole stockholder of Northfront Realtors, Inc. He had a $180,000-house in Wilmette. He had a beautiful, impeccably upper-middle-class wife, ten years his junior, whom he had married in 1953. They had no children. Sometimes Fred Sander suspected it was his fault. He had read somewhere that prolonged fear and tension could render a man sterile.

Sometimes he cursed himself for being so shortsighted. He could have arranged, back there in the early days, to set twenty or thirty thousand aside for Mason Campbell to claim on his release. Through a lawyer in a distant city—some way—there must have been some way he could have done it without much risk. But at the time it hadn't seemed that way. It had been too easy to put it off, put it off, find excuses, make more promises.

And then, finally, it had become truly impossible. He suddenly had too much money, had become too important a figure. He couldn't afford the smallest risk, and neither could he afford to let Mason Campbell get any strange ideas about claiming half the total assets of Northfront Realtors, Inc.

It had just happened. He had never planned it that way. But over the years he had slowly shut Mason Campbell entirely out of his life. And the strange thing was that the more he shut him out, the more he intruded. In different ways. Campbell had changed. He was no longer the grinning reckless youth Sander had known in the Army. The Campbell that haunted Sander's dreams now was a snarling vicious killer, a monomaniac who thirsted only for revenge.

Fred Sander remembered the first time he had ever seen Mason Campbell. Sander had come from repple depple, joining Campbell's outfit in Normandy. He wasn't Fred Sander then, of course. He was Fred Simpson. And it wasn't *Campbell's* outfit. Campbell was only a buck sergeant. Twenty-one years old. But at twenty-one he had more combat experience than any other two men in the company, and in a sense it *was* Campbell's outfit.

Fred had been twenty-five, a most reluctant draftee. Campbell had looked at him with those arrogant silvery eyes and Fred had, despite himself, tried to assume something resembling a military posture.

80

"Relax," Campbell had told him, grinning. "You don't even salute the Colonel out here."

Actually, the worst of the fighting was over, Fred soon learned. The whole division was moving now, through the hedgerows, very fast, mopping up, rolling toward Germany. Mason Campbell had already won his medals. Not that you'd have known it from talking to him.

"He's a crazy son," a Corporal Stone told Fred, wonderingly. "Big as he is, you'd think he'd be a natural target. But I seen him run right up to a bunker once. Right *through* machine-gun fire. Shoved a grenade in a gun port. And he was cold sober."

"Is that what he got decorated for?"

"I don't know. I doubt it. As I remember, he got the Silver Star for capturing a command post down in Sicily." Stone laughed. "They was going to give him a battlefield commission for that one, only the next day he got busted down to private for stealing four cases of Scotch out of the officers' mess and getting half the company plus fourteen Italian prisoners drunker'n skunks."

Fred might, and often did, dream about himself involved in such grand-style exploits, but that was as far as it had ever gone. Fred was more the skulker. He could move effectively under cover of darkness or when he was sure no one was watching. He could have stolen the Scotch, but then he'd have hidden it and sold it a bottle at a time. He knew there was no possibility of his ever jumping a bunker full of Germans. But it was the kind of thing he dreamed of doing—and so it was not strange that Mason Campbell soon became his idol. He tried to copy Campbell's swinging walk, and he wore his hat square on his head the way Campbell did.

He even started thinking of himself as a brave and reckless man. And when the day came that he was put to the test, he managed for a few minutes and to his everlasting amazement to act like one.

He and Campbell and two other soldiers were on patrol. They hadn't seen a German in four days and they had gotten careless. They approached the roofless house carelessly, bunched up, and when the machine gun cut loose, the other two soldiers were killed in their tracks. Campbell was knocked down by a bullet that hit his canteen. Fred dived backward and found cover behind a slight knoll. The ground sloped away in his favor for a considerable distance, and all he had to do was crawl backward to safety.

He risked a quick glance at the farmyard. Mason Campbell was hugging the ground behind a stone watering trough. As the machine gun ricocheted a burst off the trough, Fred realized that by the time he got back to the company for reinforcements, the Germans would have sent a man to flank Campbell while the machine gun kept him pinned.

"Fred!"

Fred didn't want to answer. He wanted to sneak back down the hill.

"Yeah?"

"Move off to the side and draw their fire."

Just like that. Draw their fire!

But he moved twenty yards to his right and poked his carbine through a bush and pulled the trigger without aiming, without even lifting his head.

Ssssp! Sssp! Wip Wap! Machine-gun bullets ripped

through the bush, showering him with twigs and leaves. He was so scared he thought his whole insides were coming right up in his throat.

He heard two loud explosions, and he heard Campbell yell.

In pure defensive terror he pointed his carbine in the general direction of the farmhouse and fired till the clip was empty.

"Got 'em!" It was Campbell's voice, hoarsely triumphant.

Fred lifted his dazed head. Campbell was standing in the farmhouse door, his carbine at the ready. Behind him a dead German hung limply across the sill of a shattered window.

The crazy fool! I didn't know he was going to run *at* the house!

"Only the three of 'em," Campbell said. "Come on!"

Fred pumped strength into his knees and slowly staggered to his feet.

Campbell was grinning, talking louder than usual, exhilarating in the joy of being alive. "He'd have got me, Fred. Sure as hell."

And that was the way Fred earned Mason Campbell's respect and gratitude. By shooting a carbine with his eyes shut and hitting a German he didn't even know existed.

But of course he never let on. He swaggered up to Campbell and shook his hand, and he swaggered along behind him for the rest of the war, convincing everyone but himself that he was indeed the dead-shot cold-nerved warrior that Mason made him out to be.

83

When the war was over he followed Campbell and his young British wife to Florida. He had discovered that he needed Campbell. He felt more like a man when he was tagging along behind Campbell. Campbell's pretty young wife didn't like him, and once or twice Campbell himself had looked at him with a puzzled frown. But Mason Campbell, Fred had come to understand, was a man who paid his debts.

Things were tough in Florida after the war. Campbell had gone down there on a job promise from some blowhard captain he had served under. But then it turned out that the captain himself couldn't get a job.

Campbell wasn't so effective on civvy street as he had been in the Army. He couldn't run a lathe, he couldn't keep books, he couldn't weld, couldn't sell, buy, barter, or manipulate. And he couldn't smash a weasel-eyed personnel manager in the mouth with a rifle butt. He needed $60 a week to pay his rent and keep his wife in English muffins. He was making $43.50 pumping gas in a service station. His wife was pregnant. He asked for a raise, and in the ensuing argument knocked the station manager into the grease pit.

Fred was doing a little better. He had hooked up with the local numbers operation—they called it the *bolita* in Florida, but it was still the numbers and it was an operation Fred understood.

He invited Campbell in.

Campbell gave him that silvery stare and said he guessed not.

Fred tried to lend him money. Campbell said No.

Fred brought him a bottle of booze. Campbell shrugged and accepted that. He had just been fired from a job picking oranges. Talk about your hotheads, Fred thought. Here's a guy still wearing his old fatigue jacket because he can't afford to buy clothes, and he can't even hold a job picking oranges!

Mason Campbell lived in a constant boiling rage. Exactly what he was mad at, Fred never did find out. He seemed utterly unable to cope with the polite pressures of civilian life. The Army's ruined him, Fred thought. He still thinks he ought to be able to get anything he wants just by running straight at it and maybe lobbing a grenade ahead of him. He doesn't understand that you've got to give a little to get a little. You've got to wheel and deal, butter up the boss when he's looking and put your hand in the till when he turns his head.

Campbell was too honest, too brutally honest. He scared people and made them angry. He was hitting the jug pretty heavy these days, too. If he wasn't careful he was going to wind up on skid row—one of those belligerent battered bums whose world came to an end the day they received their honorable discharge.

And it was then that Fred came up with the idea of the bank job. Or rather, stole the idea from a small-time heist man who had actually cased the bank but would never have the guts to go through with it and was now doing it vicariously, with a whisky bottle and a loud mouth.

But it would be easy, Fred realized. Especially for a man who had charged a bunker single-handed it would be easy. This was what Mason Campbell had been born for. He was too honest to steal, but that didn't mean he was too honest to rob a bank!

The holdup itself had been the easiest part of it. The

hard part, for Fred anyway, had been the days preceding the robbery. He had almost backed out a dozen times.

Campbell had been cold and savage. Once committed, he was entirely committed. No booze now. He had gone straight at that bank without a worry in the world. Would have gone without a mask, the crazy fool, if Fred hadn't pointed out how easy he would be to identify.

But something had happened. Maybe a secret alarm. When he and Mason walked out the door, Mason with the submachine gun, cool and unhurried, Fred with the bag of money, sweating and full of fear—when they came out the door, the first cruiser was skidding to a stop right in front of them. The cops weren't exactly sure what was happening during that first instant, and Mason Campbell could very easily have blown them clear out of the world.

You never heard that part of it later, Fred thought. The cops had been sitting ducks and Mason had let them live.

Why? Who knows! The blue uniforms, maybe. Too bad those city cops weren't dressed in Wehrmacht green. Campbell might have killed both of them by instinct.

And then the bad part.

Fred shook his head violently. It was all over. Over and done years ago. The thing to do was stop *thinking* about it. He had troubles enough, what with his wife wanting to adopt a kid, which would be fine except that he could never stand the investigation. And his secretary trying to talk him into something with those bugging green eyes. And his salesmen blowing cigar smoke in his face all day long while they explained how the last prospect had got away.

Fred Sander's stomach hurt. On top of everything else he was afraid he was getting an ulcer. So to hell with Mason Campbell. Mason Campbell was nothing compared to the problems he faced every day right in his office.

He leaned back in his padded swivel chair.

So come on anytime you're ready, he told the shade of Mason Campbell. You were a big boy once, but you'll be a broken-down ex-con when you get out, my friend. And if you come looking for me, you'll wish you'd never found me.

It was a brave speech. Fred Sander snapped off everything but the night light and opened his office door. But he poked his head out and glanced quickly both ways before he stepped into the corridor.

CHAPTER SEVEN

Mason Campbell had eaten a good breakfast, and as he stepped into the yard he exulted in the never-ending wonder of being a free man.

No wall stood between him and the horizon. No man in an office, flipping through records, had the power to tell him where he would sleep that night or where he would work the next day. He was bound only by his own will, his own desires, his own sense of responsibility and duty and decency. It was, he realized clearly, the first time in his life he had ever been truly free. The short period between the Army and prison didn't count. He had been an innocent, expecting to find virtue always rewarded, expecting to be taken at his own sense of his own worth. Totally unprepared for the complexity and hypocrisy of civilian life, he had quickly become a slave to his own helpless rage.

Not that he was a lot better suited for certain aspects of civilian life now, he admitted to himself. He doubted that he would ever make a satisfactory nine-to-fiver, working for wages or salary. Which was all right, as long as he was aware of it. If he had learned anything in prison it was to accept the reality of what *was*—and Mason Campbell *was,* just as George Peabody *was.* And it was as futile for either of them to try to be something else as for a canary to try to be a crow. The point, at least as Mason Campbell now saw it, was to try to live within the limits of your own nature, but to do it without violating the limits of other similar or dissimilar natures that abutted and surrounded you.

It wasn't that simple, of course. And one of the things that made it complicated was the unwillingness or inability of other people to believe that you *wanted* it to be that simple.

George Peabody, for example, would not believe that Mason wanted him and Sara to stay on at the farm. George would not believe that Mason was eternally grateful for the care they had taken of Ming. George would not believe that Mason wanted to raise birds, intended to make his living raising birds. Mason's very existence seemed, somehow, to irritate and worry and perhaps frighten George Peabody, and nothing Mason had been able to say or do had made the slightest difference.

Mase shrugged and lighted his after-breakfast cigarette. George Peabody would have to work out his own salvation. Mase hoped he could do it without hurting Sara too badly in the process. Mase liked Sara. He thought she deserved better than George Peabody, but he realized also that George probably fitted nicely into some special place within the limits of Sara's nature, and Mase knew you had to let those things alone.

The August sun was already serving notice that today

would be another scorcher. After the years in the South, Mase no longer minded heat. The coming winter might be a different story. He remembered the way the farm had looked on those long-ago December mornings as he had swung the big coal shovel into drifted snow, cutting paths from house to outbuildings. Stars diamond-bright in the predawn sky, snow brittle underfoot, the icicle hanging from the lip of the yard pump, the cold biting through his melton jacket and knitted earlapper cap.

In those days the barn had always been warm, or comparatively warm, from the heat generated by the cows and horses. But it was a cinch the Ford truck and George's Pontiac wouldn't keep the barn warm this winter, and Mase wondered how much heat he would have to supply for his birds. They could stand surprising extremes of cold as long as they were protected from the wind, but he wanted to avoid the problems of frozen drinkers, and he would definitely need heat if he expected to do any early breeding.

Before attending to his own birds he ambled over to the chicken run and watched Sara's small flock of Leghorns scratching in the bare dirt. The hens were Sara's, she could do with them as she pleased. Next spring he would get some poultry of his own—but they wouldn't be Leghorns or Rhode Island Reds. He wanted silkies and Andalusians and Seabrights and four or five kinds of Bantams. He would raise chickens for the sake of the *chickens,* though there would be plenty of eggs, too. But you didn't manage fancy poultry the way you did commercial stock. And then he wanted some ducks and geese—mandarins and barnacles and red-breasted. Might have to wait a while for the red-breasted; last ad he'd

90

seen they ran around two hundred a pair. And later maybe some nene.

A shadow zipped across the yard and the hens reacted in instant terror, scurrying wildly for nonexistent cover. Looking up, Mase caught the short-tailed, broad-winged silhouette of a hawk, slanting down the edge of an invisible thermal.

Why did the hens fear the hawk shadow? Mase puzzled over it. One of the first principles of genetics was that acquired traits were never passed on to the next generation. But chickens were born with the fear of the hawk silhouette—and surely that fear must have been acquired, through experience, by ancestral generations of chickens. It was almost impossible to believe that hawk-fear had been induced suddenly by a mutated gene and had then spread by natural selection through the whole world of chickens. It was a too-pat answer, designed by biologists to cover a mystery, and Mase couldn't buy it.

Why would a hand-raised canary that had never seen its mother's nest unhesitatingly construct the identical cup-shaped receptacle for its own eggs when it reached the breeding age? Why didn't it try to build a dome like the weaver finch, or sew two leaves together like the tailorbird?

Lysenko may have been temporarily discredited, Mase thought, but the battle was far from over. Some acquired traits *could* be transmitted genetically—a man would have to be blind to deny it. He looked forward to the day he could talk it over with somebody who had really studied the whole subject. But in the meantime he had other work to do.

First he fed his birds and checked their new automatic

watering system. Then he stood for a while in the sweet-smelling barn and simply watched the canaries. It was one of his great pleasures. The miraculous beauty of a bird in flight, the bright inquisitive eye, the cheerful whole-hearted acceptance of life in the present moment. Mase knew better than to anthropomorphize, to confuse bird-qualities with human-qualities; the birds had their ways and he had his ways, and one of his ways was to stand quiet, and watch. At these times he never thought of them in terms of dollars—did not in fact even want to think of selling them.

"But we can't support each other with mutual admiration," he told them, aloud. It was a habit he had picked up during the years he had lived alone. Talking to the birds. Ming had heard him one day and had tactfully refrained from comment. Mase grinned, remembering.

Then he caught up a dozen of his wildest young males and installed them singly in small show cages, which he carried out of the barn to a bench he had set up with planks and sawhorses in a shady spot. Most of the birds fluttered wildly back and forth, unable at first even to locate the perches in their new and strangely restricted surroundings. He gave them a chance to settle down, then moved slowly toward them with his hands out. Again the birds fluttered in panic. He repeated this maneuver over and over till finally they realized the hands were no threat. They sat quietly now as he approached—all but one, a ticked frost, that had become completely disoriented and now huddled on the cage bottom, breathing heavily through its open beak. Mase returned this bird to the barn, first jotting its band number in his notebook.

Next he whipped a long-billed green cap from his pocket, set it squarely on his head and thrust his face close to the cages. Again the birds went into a mild frenzy. It took longer to get them to accept the cap. Most birds just didn't like hats for some bird reason of their own. Mase put the cap on backward, and he had the bill sticking out over his right ear when he heard someone cough behind him and whirled to see Libby Dean staring at him with eyes round as half-dollars, and a mouth to match.

"I . . . ah . . . Sara thought Ming might be out here with you."

"Ming went on a picnic with Billy What's-his-name. Early this morning."

"Oh. Well, I was on my way to Columbus and I just thought she might like to come along." Libby smiled brightly.

She's not a bad-looking woman, Mase was thinking. But she's got that bossy schoolteachery way about her.

Libby flushed when he didn't answer.

"Well, just tell her I stopped by." She turned to go.

"Bought your bird yet?"

Libby stopped. Looked at him over her shoulder. "No, I . . . I changed my mind."

"Decision like that takes a lot of thought," Mase agreed.

Again Libby flushed. "Now what's that supposed to mean?"

"Nothing." Mase grinned.

"All right. So I was being nosy." Libby turned to face him. "Ming is a very outstanding student, Mr. Campbell. I have high hopes for her."

"I have hopes for her myself," Mase said.

"Do you?" Libby bit her lip. "Oh, of course you do! You know—it just dawned on me how *I'd* feel if some nibby schoolteacher came poking around my place."

"That's all right. Can't say I blame you—under the circumstances."

"It's not because . . . because of your background," Libby said quickly. "I want you to understand that, Mr. Campbell."

"In other words, you're not prejudiced against ex-convicts."

"You don't want to make it easy, do you?" Libby took a breath. "No, I'm not prejudiced against ex-convicts—but since you insist on being blunt, I'll tell that I *am* prejudiced against people who put birds in cages." She stared at him curiously. "It's especially surprising to me that *you* would deprive any living creature of its freedom."

"You got a point there," Mase said. "But not a very good one. You want me to turn these birds loose? They'd all be dead in a week, and if one of them did learn to forage for himself, he'd never survive the winter."

"Which only proves that Nature never intended a bird to live in a cage!"

"Never intended chickens to live in a henhouse either, did she?"

"I think that's a rather ridiculous comparison."

"Yeah, I suppose it is. Any fool knows that Nature created the jungle fowl so it'd end up fifty thousand years later as chicken-in-a-basket. And minks to keep city women warm while they walk across the sidewalk from the taxi to the theater. And golden hamsters to live in laboratories with silver needles in their brains.

94

"But birds now, that's something different. Birds were created to fly free—unless, of course, they happen to have pretty feathers for the ladies' hats or good thick meat for the table, or unless they help themselves to the farmers' corn, or make a mess on the courthouse steps. And then we'll shoot 'em and trap 'em and poison 'em by the millions. It's perfectly all right to kill birds—but to catch one or breed one and put him in a cage and feed him and take care of him and enjoy him and give him a chance to enjoy himself while he's living five times as long as he would in the wild—why, that's immoral, my good man, and a crime against Nature!"

Mase's voice was intense, his face alive with anger. "That's nothing but stinking hypocrisy and it makes me sick to my stomach."

Libby eyed him cautiously. "There's something in what you say," she admitted. "But you know as well as I do that mankind isn't going to stop killing chickens and minks."

"I don't say they should. I'm no fanatic. All I want is to raise my birds in peace without some sentimental fool moralizing at me."

"Well, thank you very much! I may be a fool, but nobody ever accused me of being overly sentimental. And I still don't see any sense in keeping little birds in cages."

"The sense of it is hard to argue. And I apologize for calling you names." He grinned. "Maybe I *am* a fanatic in a way, because I'm pretty well convinced that in another fifty years or so there'll be very few birds left in this country—except for the ones in cages."

"Oh, I doubt that."

"You do, eh? Did you ever hear of the nene goose, Miss Dean?"

She shook her head dubiously.

"It's the state bird of Hawaii now. Only place in the world it ever existed. Big handsome gray honker, non-migratory, doesn't like water. Used to be thousands of them in Hawaii, then the Westerners started slaughtering them for food, and all of a sudden the nene were gone. During a period in the 1940's there were no wild nene sighted, but it happened that a man in Hawaii, name of Michael C. Stanley, had decided long before that the nene should be saved. He caught up a pair and tried to breed them in confinement—succeeded, too, but with one thing and another never managed to build up a big flock. At the low point, in 1946, he had eleven nene geese on his ranch, and it's quite possible those were the last eleven nene in the world.

"Then in 1951 the Wildfowl Trust in England somehow got interested. Sent a man to Hawaii and talked Mike Stanley out of a pair of his precious geese. Turned out later that both birds were female, so Stanley had to send a gander by air to England. But those three birds got right down to business in England, and in 1952 they reared nine young nene. By 1954 they had raised the world population to sixty-eight. Two years later it was up to one hundred fifty. They started shipping birds back to Hawaii and releasing them in the old nesting grounds. Some of these birds have taken hold, but it's still touch and go whether the nene can ever reestablish itself as a wild species.

"The point is, though, that the nene will not die out. The English outfit has over a hundred now, and they're beginning to ship pairs to reliable breeders all over the world. If I'm lucky, in a year or two I might be able to latch on to a pair myself."

"I'd never heard that," Libby said slowly.

"Lots of things people never hear. Or don't pay attention to when they do. We used to have a bird called the Carolina Parrakeet, only parrot-type bird native to this country, ranged all over the South. We destroyed it—same as we did the passenger pigeon. Today our bluebird population is way down, and lots of our waterfowl—I could name a dozen species. Our birds are disappearing, and except for a few conservation nuts, nobody seems to care. But we'll care someday, Miss Dean. When the birds are gone we'll wake up to what we've lost and we'll care then, but it'll be too late."

"Well, yes," she said in a subdued voice. "I know we're losing birds. You don't even see the robins and the wrens you used to when I was a little girl." She looked at Mase with a new expression. "But I didn't know you were interested in that aspect of it."

"I'm interested in birds. Goldfinch or golden eagle. In his own way one's as good as another. Someday I hope to breed bluebirds here, and mockingbirds and kingfishers and the rare warblers. And everything else that's getting scarce and a lot that aren't scarce at all. I want to have a thousand finches flying loose in an aviary as big as a house. I'll have Chinese painted quail and Amherst pheasants and partridges coming up underfoot like grasshoppers. But I'll be doing it because I want to do it, and it won't make me a bit more important or worthwhile than if I stuck to Red Factor canaries."

Libby looked stunned. "I had no idea . . . I mean it

might not be more important to you. . . . But it just opens a whole new door. . . ." She shook her head in wonder. "Ming never mentioned——"

"Look. Ming doesn't know anything about it. I've never shot my mouth off like this to anybody. The whole thing may fall through—so do me a favor and forget I mentioned it. Will you do that, Miss Dean?"

"I won't forget," she said, smiling. "But I won't tell anyone"—she hesitated—"if you'll stop calling me Miss Dean. Is that a bargain?"

Mase opened his eyes. "Sure. What do you want me to call you?"

"My name is Libby." She flushed. "I mean, my pupils call me Miss Dean five hundred times a day and I get so *tired* of it."

"Sure," Mase said softly. He was suddenly aware of her in a totally different way. As Miss Dean she was Ming's schoolteacher—a handsome but slightly waspish young woman. As Libby she was something else again. A pretty thing, with a full soft mouth and gray-green eyes that changed expression from moment to moment. He smelled her light perfume. And felt something burst into life within him.

She stepped back, her eyes widening. "What were you doing with these birds when I came up? With your hat on sideways and waving your arms and everything."

"Training them to stand steady at the show."

He was peering deeply into her eyes, searching for . . . searching for what? It had been fifteen years since he last probed a woman's eyes, and at some point in that passage of time he had very nearly succeeded in wiping

98

the intimate memory of women's eyes from his mind. When he walked out of prison the women had been there, of course, all around him, the streets full of them. Soft warm flesh under thin nylon. But he had avoided them. Had avoided looking into their eyes. Why?

His chest was tight. The skin of his face felt stretched and burning. Involuntarily, he reached out and touched Libby's arm.

She jumped away with a startled gasp.

He was after her instantly. Not thinking. His body pursuing her body. He caught her as easily as the hawk catches the field mouse. One big hand on each of her arms, between shoulder and elbow. He held her for a moment, almost lifting her feet off the ground, peering blindly down into her face.

"Let me go!"

He bent to her mouth. Pressed his mouth to her mouth. Kissed her . . . fifteen years . . . kissed her soft warm lips . . . and the fifteen years tumbled in upon themselves and became as fifteen days. Became as a day, an hour—became nothing at all.

He was Mason Campbell. He was holding a woman in his arms. He lifted his mouth. And looked at her. He wanted to tell her——

"Let me *go!* I'll scream for Sara!"

"Sara can't help you now," Mase said. But he was smiling. He felt very good. He released his grip on Libby Dean's arms.

She staggered, almost fell against him. He put out his hand to catch her elbow and she jumped away from him.

"*Well!*" She was breathing in deep gasps. Her blouse had pulled up out of her skirt. Her smooth blond hair was disheveled. Her face was redder than Mase's best bird. She stepped back, a safe distance.

"I thought bird lovers were *gentle* people!"

"I'm sorry," Mase said.

"Oh yes! You certainly sound it."

"Well, maybe in a way I'm not." He laughed. "But I won't do it again," he said quickly, seriously. "I mean, not you. I mean you don't have to be afraid of me."

"I'm not afraid of you!" She was angry, getting angrier by the minute. She tucked in her blouse. Her hands were shaking.

"Hey, I really do apologize," Mase said, becoming alarmed. "I don't know what came over me."

"Never mind!" She shook her head in exasperation, then patted ineffectually at her flying hair. "I'm a big grown-up girl, Mr. Campbell, and I've been kissed before—so please don't worry about it."

"Okay," Mase said, blinking.

She turned and headed for her car, making hard work of it in her heels over the uneven ground. She kept her head high, and the last he saw of her was her stiff, indignant back as she rounded the far corner of the barn.

CHAPTER EIGHT

Toward the middle of October a freak cold front moved unexpectedly from Canada down across the Great Lakes into Ohio. At ten o'clock in the morning the thermometer registered sixty degrees under cloudy skies; at noon came a violent storm with high winds and hail; by three in the afternoon the front had passed, the skies were crystal clear, the temperature had dropped twenty degrees, and the weather bureau was predicting heavy frost during the night.

Mase was worried about his birds. Heating the barn had turned out to be a fairly complicated problem. The only practical solution was to partition off and insulate the bird section. But his money was running low, and there was no use putting up wall board if he couldn't afford to buy the heaters. So he had reluctantly decided to postpone any construction till after the show.

"It's not the cold itself," he told Ming as they checked the birds that afternoon. "A little cold won't hurt 'em.

But if it warms up again in a few days, it's liable to throw them into a partial molt. They're not used to these sudden changes. And if they molt now, we can just forget about the show."

"Why don't we bring them in the house?"

"By God, why not! That's what I call a *real* bird-keeper's idea."

Since he didn't want to crowd them unnecessarily, he decided to transfer fifty of the best to the available cages. And Ming found out that setting up cages for fifty birds took a little doing. She and Mase worked side by side, cutting newspapers for the bottoms, fitting perches, filling seed cups. Then Mase had to pick out the probable winners, and that took more time. When Sara called them for supper, the barn lights had been on for an hour and Mase had stocked only about a quarter of the cages.

"We'll grab a quick bite and then finish up," he said.

"All right." It was cold in the barn, even with Ming's heavy sweater on. She liked working with her father, but birds could be aggravating, there was no doubt of that, and she sometimes wondered if they could possibly be worth the trouble Mase went to. One thing was sure: The darned birds didn't *appreciate* anything you did for them. The canary Mase wanted was invariably the canary he couldn't catch, and then when he did get it in the cage, the ungrateful thing would sometimes sulk, or maybe tear into its cagemate, and then Mase would have to separate them and try to find two or three who could get along together.

As Ming and her father entered the kitchen, each carrying two cages, Sara pushed her lips out but held her peace. At this stage of the game she could have found her refrigerator full of frosted canaries and been no more than mildly surprised.

George was late and she wasn't going to wait on him, Sara said, ladling Mase's plate full of chicken and dumplings.

"I don't hardly see how a man like you can stand to eat a chicken," Sara said.

"Doesn't bother me as long as you get the feathers off. I just pretend I'm eating tuna fish." It was Sara's favorite joke, and he never told her he was tired of it, because even old jokes were better than the nervous formality with which she had treated him the first few weeks. The only trouble with Sara was that she wanted the whole hog or none. Once she had lost her early fear she began asking him, straight out, questions that even Ming avoided.

Did he know where the other man was? Did he ever think about trying to get even? Or about the money? Who *was* that other man, anyway?

She actually asked him that.

There isn't any other man, Mase had told her in some heat.

And then she had whipped out that detective magazine, and there it was: the story and the picture and his name. Not fifteen years ago and over and done with, but right here, now, at this time and in this house.

"Why didn't you tell them who it was?" Sara had asked.

"It doesn't matter now, Sara. Forget about it, will you please? And throw that damned magazine away!"

"No, it doesn't matter now," she had answered quietly.

"But ten years ago it mattered, Mason. When Ming was little. It might have mattered . . . if you had come home then . . . not to you maybe, but to Ming—and to your father."

Mase had walked away from her. She hadn't mentioned it again. He had thought about it a great many times since. And it was funny thing: In all those fifteen years he had never thought about it in quite that way. And maybe it was just as well he had never thought about it that way. It wouldn't have changed anything, except that the fifteen years would then have been impossible instead of merely hard.

But it had been there in the back of his mind all the time, he realized now. And it had done something to him. He wasn't sure what. But it had tightened him somehow and turned him in upon himself. Maybe the birds had kept him sane. The thought caught him by surprise, and he was examining it when he became aware that Ming was talking to him and staring at him curiously, and with an effort he brought himself back to the supper table.

"What did you say?" He was trying to picture her at the age of five.

"Nothing important." She shook her head, laughing. "You were a million miles away."

Only a thousand miles—and fifteen years, he thought.

They heard a car in the driveway.

"That's George, and he better have a good story," Sara said grimly.

They waited for what seemed a long time—till George came in rubbing his hands and blowing his breath to show it was cold outside. Like maybe he was a woodchopper, Ming thought, who'd been at hard labor all through a bitter day and was now coming home to his well-earned supper.

"How's things at the Lakeview?" Sara said.

George scowled, then looked at Mase. "Women don't understand what a man's got to go through if he wants to do business." He was in one of his expansive moods, Ming saw. They had been coming more frequently lately. "Just like a city man has to belong to the country club. Why, there's more deals turned right there at the Lakeview than in all the offices in town put together."

"Yes indeedy," Sara said. "You give Herman Strohmeyer a quarter and he gives you a bottle of beer. Big deal!"

Aunt Sara was getting pretty tart with Uncle George lately, Ming thought. Used to be she'd just listen to his big talk and pretend she believed it.

George shot his wife a glance that had knives in it, but Sara, safe behind the armor of the righteous, just smirked.

"Bert Bradley tells me the FBI's still interested in you, Mase," George said with surprising boldness.

Ming's fork stopped halfway to her mouth. In the sudden silence she could hear the canaries chirping in the kitchen where Mase had left them.

"Got birds in the house now, have we?" George said.

"You don't mind, do you, George?" Mase's voice was soft, polite.

"No, no. It's your house, Mase. You wanta put a cow

in the parlor, I'll help you bed her down." George snickered.

Mase stared at him. George busied himself with his dumplings, refusing to meet Mase's gaze.

And I don't blame him, Ming thought. When her father stared at you that way—the blue-silver eyes narrow and glinting like lake ice in the sun—well, you either had to look away or else go ahead and make something out of it. He never stared at *her* that way, and she hoped he never would.

Mase pushed back his chair. "Ready?"

Ming swallowed and nodded.

"Excuse us," Mase said politely to Sara. Then his hard face relaxed and he smiled. "Good supper, even if you did make me feel like a cannibal."

She returned his smile, but her heart wasn't in it.

Ming grabbed her parka from the hook behind the door and went out through the kitchen ahead of her father. As she stepped into the yard she thought at first that somebody had turned a light on. A bright red light.

"No, *no!*" She had never heard her father cry out like that. He went past her in a great leap. She ran after him. The yard was bright as day. Then the heat hit her, as though somebody had opened a huge furnace door, and she saw the flames. The whole end of the barn was a sheet of fire. Her father was running straight at it, through heat that even at this distance made Ming put her hand in front of her face.

"Call the fire department!" Mase bellowed back at her. She saw him veer to the side, away from the flames, and race around the corner of the barn, his long legs carrying him over the ground at astonishing speed. She wanted to follow him. But she tore back to the house, through the kitchen, burst into the dining room—screaming.

"The barn's on fire!"

Sara and George were up in an instant, Sara to the phone, dialing frantically, George running back and forth, cursing, his little brown eyes bugging out of his head.

"Oh, the poor birds!" Ming flew through the kitchen, out into the yard again. She could hear the fire now—crackling, roaring. The yard was hot. The barn was twice as high as it should be—nothing but red and yellow flames, shooting high into the still night sky.

Thank God there was no wind. Maybe the house wouldn't catch.

She ran toward the side of the barn where her father had disappeared, and as she rounded the corner she saw that there was still hope. It wasn't as bad as it looked from the front. Not yet. Only the end of the barn was afire—the rest of it apparently untouched. But the whole barn was hot! She could feel the heat coming off the dry wood as though the whole barn were one immense radiator.

The windows . . . she came to the windows. They were dark. The lights must have gone out. There was only a dim red smoky glow through the windows. And they were broken—she saw now. Most of them were smashed—great gaping holes in those fine windows her father had worked so hard to build.

"Daddy! *Dad!*" She screamed at the top of her lungs. "Are you in there?"

No answer. Only the growing roar of the fire.

Then another window crashed into a million fragments of flying glass—and Mason Campbell poked his head out. He was coughing, gasping. In the darkness his face looked deathly white. He saw Ming.

"Here!" He shoved a bird cage out the window. "Move 'em back where they can get air!" Ming jumped forward to take the cage, and stumbled over other cages on the ground.

"I think the smoke's got most of 'em," Mase said, strangely calm. "I'll tear the flights open—maybe they'll make it out the windows."

He vanished again in the flickering red smoke.

Ming breathlessly carried the cages to the other side of the henhouse, a hundred feet from the barn. She made three trips. It seemed almost a waste of time. The birds were dead—all but one or two—lying motionless on the cage bottoms, eyes closed. But when she put the last cages down she saw that a few of the other birds had recovered, at least partially, and were huddled on the perches.

Hurrying to the barn again, she found the windows red now—the fire was spreading inside. There were dead birds all over the ground. Her father thrust his head out the window. She could see him plainly. Hair matted down across his forehead, face streaked and dripping with sweat. He shoveled a double handful of birds out on the grass. Then he tossed a cage to Ming, and another and another.

"Put 'em in the cages. Maybe they'll come to."

He sounded hopeless, though. And as she picked the limp bodies of the birds off the cold ground she felt that it was really a futile gesture. She piled them into the cages. Occasionally she felt one quiver, but most of them were surely dead. It broke her heart. The birds were so little and so soft and they hadn't done anything to deserve this. One minute they had been the happiest birds in the world and now they were scattered like dead leaves in the frosty grass.

She lifted her head at a sudden roar and saw streamers of bright yellow fire shoot out the broken windows. The draft from the windows was sucking the fire all through the inside of the barn.

"Come out!" she screamed. "Daddy! Come *out!*"

Amazingly, a cluster of birds, redder than the fire, zoomed out the windows. Five—six—a dozen—flying strongly as they disappeared in the darkness overhead. Then Mase at the window, pitching more dead birds toward Ming. The flames leaping madly behind him. He looked like a man standing on the edge of Hell.

He turned his head back toward the fire . . . hesitated. A tongue of flame wrapped itself around his body. Ming screamed. And Mase dived forward, arching through the window like a diver coming off a springboard. He tumbled head over heels and lay for an instant on his back, staring blindly into the night sky.

Ming dropped to her knees at his head. She took his face in her hands. He gave her a twisted grin. "I'm all right," he said quietly.

She sobbed in relief.

He scrambled immediately to his feet, casting about on the ground for the last canaries.

"Some of them flew out," she said.

He nodded. Flames were shooting from the windows now, and the walls of the barn were erupting in red holes as the fire burned through. As they watched, a ball of fire shot out through one of the windows like a meteor. But it didn't fall in the curve of an exploding spark. It soared upward . . . up . . . up . . . faltered, hung suspended in the sky, dropped at their feet, a smoking blackened thing.

Mason crushed it violently underfoot. *"Damn* it." His voice was harsh. Harsh.

The wail of a siren in the distance. Growing louder. The pounding rattle of Blairsville's ancient fire truck, black-slickered volunteer firemen clinging to it like beetles. Then the string of cars—firemen who had missed the truck, and the merely curious, the firebuffs who would get out of a warm bed and drive thirty miles in the middle of the night to see something burn.

The creaking pumper coughed up a thin fitful stream that had no more effect on the fire than a garden hose. The firemen stood around with their helmets pushed back. There was nothing to be done. With no wind blowing, the barn burned straight up, the flames mounting higher and higher into the sky until for a moment the whole barn seemed made of fire. And then it collapsed upon itself in a geyser of sparks, and there was nothing but a glowing mass of coals—and the firemen running about the yard dousing stray embers.

Mase and Ming had carried the cages full of birds into the house, stacking them in the warmth of the kitchen.

"Oh, the poor poor things," Sara said. "Do you think a drop of whiskey would revive them, Mason?"

"Might."

He looked like the wrath of God, Ming thought. His eyes, usually so clear and brilliant, were bloodshot and red-rimmed. He had a nasty gash on his forehead and the blood had run down the side of his face, drying in a crusty brown streak. She wanted to clean and bandage it, but he shook his head absently.

Sara found a bottle with an inch of her cooking whiskey in the bottom. Mason diluted it with water, tried to administer it by beak with an eyedropper. Of the first six birds he picked up, five were obviously dead. He put them in a paper sack, his face emotionless.

"You try the rest of 'em," he told Ming, standing up and handing her the eyedropper. "I've got to see a fella." His voice was flat and far away. He went out the door.

"You do it!" Ming gave the eyedropper to Sara. "I'm afraid he——"

Sara nodded. "Yes. Go after him. I'll tend to the poor birdies."

In the yard Ming was momentarily confused. So many people milling about. So much loud talk. Then she saw her father, head and shoulders towering over most of the others. She ran toward him. Sheriff Sam Dunbar was talking to him. But he was already moving away. The sheriff called to him. Mase gave no sign that he had heard. He circled a group of men, peering into their faces, moved on to the next—and here he stopped.

"Like to have a word with you," he said to one of them.

As the man looked up, Ming saw it was Uncle George, his face round and white and strange under the big black fireman's helmet.

"Why sho, Mase," George said. "I was just telling Bert here——"

"Alone," Mase said.

George hunched his shoulders. Two of the men near him stepped away a few feet. Now it was George and Bert Bradley facing her father. Bert wasn't wearing his deputy's uniform—he had on a big sheepskin coat and a wide-brimmed rancher's hat. He looked formidable, Ming thought. Almost as tall as her father and twice as bulky.

"Nothing you can't say in front of Bert, is it?" George was sullen.

"If I knew you did it on purpose . . ." Mase prodded George in the chest, hard, with his forefinger. "I'd kill you, George. And I may anyway."

"Did what?" George gasped.

Mase bent his head toward George, and the line of neck and head was frightening. Again he stabbed George in the chest with that inflexible forefinger.

"You threw a cigar butt in the barn, didn't you, George?"

"No!" George shook his head wildly. "My God—I wouldn't do anything like that, Mase!"

"Sure you would," Mase said softly. "Only you probably just threw it *at* the barn—with your head turned the other way. Because that's the kind of a gutless two-faced creep you are."

"Now take it easy, Mase," Bert Bradley said. "You're

112

accusing George of arson, which is a serious felony, and far as I can see you don't have no grounds whatsoever to make a charge like that."

Mase's head swung slowly, disbelievingly, toward the deputy.

George took a step backward, putting Bradley partly between him and Mason.

"I seen you smoking in the barn plenty of times!" His voice was ragged. "You're not going to put the blame on me for——"

It was as far as he got.

Mase shoved Bert Bradley out of his way with his left hand, and with his right hand he hit George Peabody flush in the face. It was all one motion, so incredibly quick that it was over before Ming could grasp it. George went down like a man struck by lightning. He lay flat on his back, arms outstretched, face oddly pale in the dying red glow of the fire.

"That'll be murder if he's dead, Mase," Bradley said hoarsely. "I always knew you'd come to it some day."

The two men who had moved away came running back. One knelt and pressed his ear to George's chest. "He's all right. Just knocked cold."

"Well, he could be dead easy as not. You're too free with your hands, Mase."

"And you're too free with your mouth. Now get the hell off my place before I throw you off."

Bradley threw his sheepskin coat open. Ming could see the star on his shirt pocket catch the light, and the shiny tips of the cartridges in the belt around his waist. He put his hand on the butt of his revolver.

Ming's hands flew to her mouth. She wanted to cry out, to stop this before it went any further. But her father was smiling at Bert Bradley.

The other two men stood silently, mouths agape. In the shadows beyond she sensed more men moving closer.

"You pull that pistol out and I'll shove it down your throat," her father said. His voice was calm, almost pleasant.

"Oh, you will!"

Bradley jerked the revolver out of his holster. Ming saw the deadly length of the blue-black barrel. And she saw her father move straight at Bert Bradley, and the revolver went flying in the air, and Bert Bradley grunted and doubled up and sagged slowly to his knees.

For a horrible instant she thought her father was going to kick him in the face.

"Just stand where you are, Mason!" a voice spoke sharply from the circle of onlookers. Sheriff Sam Dunbar shouldered his way between men. He stopped ten feet from Mase. He was wearing a black thigh-length leather coat, no hat; his hands were empty. He looked down at his deputy, still hunched in agony, and at George Peabody stretched on the ground but with his eyes open now and clearly conscious.

"What in Sam Hill are you trying to do, Mase?"

"Bradley poked his nose into a private argument," one of the original onlookers spoke up. "And then he pulled his gun. I'd say he was out of line."

Dunbar seemed not to hear. "You got anything to say for yourself?" he asked Mase.

"I'm not going back to jail, Sam."

114

"Knocking a deputy sheriff down ain't just the way to stay out, Mase. You know that as well as I do."

Mase stared at him warily.

Oh, please! Ming prayed. *You can get out of it now. Just back down for once. It won't hurt you!*

Bert Bradley's paralyzed diaphragm suddenly began to function again. He gulped air into his lungs, lifted his head.

"You're under arrest, Campbell," he croaked.

Mase glanced down at him as though he were a yapping bulldog.

"So I shouldn't have hit him," he said to Dunbar. "What do you want me to do, apologize?"

"No, you're not gonna apologize," Bradley grunted. He lunged forward, scrabbling in the grass, coming to his knees with the revolver in his hand. "No lousy ex-con——"

Ming screamed.

Her father's big foot, at the end of a leg that seemed seven feet long, kicked the gun as Bradley pulled the trigger.

Ba-rrrang!

The gun sailed into the air—and Mason, in a hurtling awkward leap, caught it before it hit the ground.

"All right," he said, his words as cold and hard as chunks of steel. "We'll play it your way." He pointed the gun at Bert Bradley. "On your feet."

Bradley staggered upright, hands out in supplication. "Wait, Mase! Wait!"

"Gimme that gun!" Dunbar started forward. "Are you out of your mind!"

115

"Stop right there, Sam. And keep your hands in the open. This is between me and Bert."

For a long instant nobody moved, nobody breathed. Some of the car headlights had been switched on, and the scene was outlined in stark black and white. Bradley, cowering, whimpering, eyes bulging, his sheepskin coat hanging open over his big belly—Sam Dunbar frozen, one foot advanced in mid-stride—the ring of onlookers, some in firemen's helmets, those behind Bradley scrambling for safety—her father, standing almost at his ease, facing Bert Bradley, extending the heavy black revolver slowly to arm's length, pointing it straight at the deputy's wet white face.

And from out of the black sky dropped an autumn leaf . . . fluttering down, swirling, wind-tossed. . . . But no wind blew. . . . Not a leaf . . . an autumn bird . . . hovering for a moment, confused in the glare of headlights, each feather limned in gold . . . hovering, and then closing its wings and dropping confidently to perch on the steady black barrel of the gun.

Mason stared at it in astonishment.

The bird cocked its head—bold bright eye fixed on Mason's face.

Mason jiggled the gun in sharp annoyance.

The canary flew immediately to his shoulder. Pecked his ear. Tugged at the shaggy hair on his neck.

Mason frowned. The revolver seemed to be growing too heavy for him. It was pointing at Bradley's belly, at his feet, at the ground.

No one spoke or moved.

Mason's face was unreadable. Then, with a slight

116

shrug, he turned, handed the revolver to Sam Dunbar, walked past him toward the house—bird riding easy on his shoulder.

Ming watched him go. She wanted to follow him, but her knees were so weak she couldn't move.

"You're not gonna let him get away with that!" Bradley's voice was a whisper.

"Get away with what?" Dunbar tucked the gun into his side pocket. "You didn't think he was gonna kill you, did you, Bert?"

"Why, sure he was gonna kill me!"

"If you really believe that, you oughta buy a ton of birdseed and spread it all over the county for Thanksgiving."

Some of the men laughed.

"I think he was gonna nick your ear," Dunbar said. "Or maybe he was trying to scare you to death."

"Pointing a gun at a police officer's a felony!" Bradley shouted. "You can't——"

"But you're not a police officer," Dunbar said gently. "You automatically suspended yourself when you took a shot at an unarmed man."

"You can't do that to me, Sam!"

"You did it to yourself, Bert. You can have a hearing next week in front of the board if you want it." Dunbar raised his voice. "Let's break it up, boys. Fire's out and the fun's over." He caught Ming's eye. "You better go in there and fix your daddy a cup of coffee." He smiled at her. "And give that canary bird a little something extra, too."

CHAPTER NINE

It was after midnight when the three of them—Ming, Mase, and Sara—finished ministering to the canaries. Of the hundred-odd birds Mase had salvaged, sixty-three were dead. Ten were definitely ill or badly injured. A dozen others were questionable, sitting all in a heap on the perches, feathers ruffled, eyes dull.

"Twenty-five healthy birds," Mase said. "And most of 'em hens. Not counting old Bully here." The tame brown-and-gold canary was now sleeping peacefully in a covered cage.

"Is he the same Bully? I mean the one the warden gave you?"

"Bully was his grandfather. He's the last of the line."

All during the painful process of separating the dead birds from the living, Mase had worked quietly, seldom looking up. Ming and Sara had exchanged glances over his head. The terrible violence of the fire and the fight was already like a bad dream, but the stunned birds were

118

a constant reminder of its reality, and Ming didn't know what to say or how to say it.

"Twenty-five birds," Mase repeated, covering the last of the cages and switching off the light in the dining-room. "That puts me back where I was ten years ago."

"Oh *no*—you've still got your mutation!" Ming cried. "You can raise more birds from these."

"Sure. Just a minor setback." There was no bitterness or self-pity in Mase's voice. In fact, there was nothing at all in it.

Ming glanced at him in new concern, and fear.

He grinned reassuringly. "Don't worry, honey. We'll work something out."

But she did worry, lying awake in the dark long after she went to bed. After that first blowup her father had become too calm. It wasn't natural. She'd have felt better if he had ranted and raved, or cried, or shown *some* emotion. He wasn't even curious about Uncle George. Sara had beckoned Ming into the bathroom and whispered that George had sneaked in the front door and up the stairs and thrown his clothes out the window and then lit out for parts unknown in the Pontiac.

Yes, he had asked her to go with him, Sara admitted. Maybe she'd go to him later, she said. After she got it all straight in her mind. But right now she didn't think so. She pushed her lips in and out. Her eyes were red. It was awful to find out you didn't like a man after being married to him for twenty years, she told Ming. But right now she just didn't think she could take any more of George Peabody.

Ming woke up to bright sunlight. Almost ten o'clock!

She jumped out of bed and rushed to the window before she remembered why she was sleeping so late. The desolate black ruins of the barn, clearly visible from her window, struck her vision with a sickening shock.

She hastily donned jeans and sweater, jerked a comb through her tangled hair, brushed her teeth, splashed her face with cold water, and was downstairs in record time.

"Your father's gone to town," Sara said. "Had to walk, too. I forgot all about the truck, but you can see what's left of it sticking up through the ashes out there."

"Wouldn't you know! Uncle George saved *his* car because he was too lazy to put it in the barn."

"Maybe that wasn't the only reason he saved it," Sara said darkly.

"Oh, Aunt Sara! I can't believe he set the barn on fire. Not on purpose—nobody in his right mind would do a thing like that."

"Maybe not. But I think it's just as well we can't see into each other's right minds sometimes, Ming. It might make us downright sick to our stomach."

"I suppose you're right. I've had some pretty bad thoughts I'd hate to have other people know about."

"Pshaw, child! If your kind of bad thoughts were the worst anybody ever had, this old world would be a lovely place to live."

Ming walked into the dining room, carrying her coffee. "The birds seem better, don't they?"

"Five more were dead this morning. Your daddy said their lungs are so delicate. They can't stand smoke."

"They're not exactly delicate," Ming said. "But their whole respiratory system is altogether different from ours.

120

When they breathe, the air goes right down into their hollow bones."

"Oh, pardon me! I forgot I was talking to the birdgirl of Blairsville."

Ming laughed. "I guess I *have* learned a lot. And I didn't even know it!"

"You've learned a lot about birds, but have you learned anything about your daddy? I heard he come within a whisker of killing Bert Bradley last night."

"I thought I had—until that happened. But then he was like a stranger." She stared moodily out the window. "I should be in school."

"School'll still be there tomorrow. How's Miss Fancypants Dean? Haven't seen her out here since summer."

"She's all right." Ming smiled at her aunt. "You think she's snooty, but she's not. It's just her natural way."

"Maybe so. I thought for a while there she was kind of interested in trying out for a job as your new step-mamma."

"Oh, I don't think so!" Ming felt herself blushing. "I mean they don't have anything in common—they don't even like each other."

"They've got a few things in common," Sara said tartly. "I'd say the biggest trouble with being fifteen is you think everybody over twenty-five is practically senile. Your daddy's a mighty attractive man, Ming—rough ways and all—and he's still a young man, even if he might not seem so to you."

"Well, I know that."

"Do you? Your daddy's going to come home with a wife one of these days, and it might be kind of a shock to you if you've got it in your head that love was invented special for fifteen-year-old kids like you and Billy Gabriel."

"Oh, don't be so silly, Aunt Sara! This isn't eighteen ninety. I know all about the facts of life—and I'm *not* in love with Billy Gabriel!"

When Sara didn't answer, Ming stole a glance at her. But Sara was busy with biscuit dough, apparently unintrigued by the facts of life.

It was hard for Ming to think of Aunt Sara and Uncle George as—well, as man and woman. They had always been "old" to her, but she realized suddenly that Sara wasn't really old at all. What was she . . . about forty-eight? Her face was still plump and pretty, her figure strong, if a little thick and clumsy. She must have loved Uncle George once, and she might love and be loved by another man in the years to come.

But that had nothing to do with her father and Libby Dean. My gosh, Ming thought—that'd be like a pretty young porcupine falling in love with a tough old wolf—it wouldn't happen in a million years.

"I wonder what Daddy's going to do," she said. "Isn't it funny how we can just stand here talking as though nothing had happened? And yet we both know that losing his birds was just about the worst thing in the world that could possibly happen to him."

"That's the way women are," Sara said, punching out circles of dough with her biscuit cutter. "It's what saves us from going crazy. We know, and we care—just as much as the men do or more—but we don't get all desperate and wild like they do. Maybe it's because men live

122

too much for themselves. They think the world's coming to an end when they fail or their business goes bust—but we know that the world's going right on same as always, with more babies to be born and looked after and our men to be cooked for and comforted. Just like you and I know that those little birdies in the dining room will have more babies next year, and pretty soon it won't even matter whether there was a fire or not. But your daddy, with all his knowledge about birds, doesn't know that— I mean *know* it in his bones without thinking about it, like we know it."

"Why, that's exactly right! I never understood that before."

"You *knew* it—so you didn't have to understand it." Sara slid the pan of biscuits into the oven and put her hands on her hips, palms out so she wouldn't get flour on her dress. "I don't understand it myself, but it's part of what makes the world go round."

Libby Dean had heard four different versions of the fire and the Campbell-Bradley fracas before she left the teachers' lounge for her first class, so she wasn't surprised to find Ming absent. She worried about her off and on through the day, though. She didn't pretend to know what made Mason Campbell tick, and she wondered what would happen now that his birds were gone. If the flare of violence last night was any indication, poor Ming might be in for a very bad time.

At three thirty, almost before the last student had bolted out the door, Mason Campbell walked into her classroom. He was wearing a short suede jacket and a

123

blue woolen shirt. She had never seen him wear a suit. His face looked raw, as though he had been walking all day in the cold wind. He had recently combed his hair, wetting it with water and combing it flat. But it was no improvement, she thought—it just made his face all the harder.

She stood up behind her desk, strangely no more secure here on her home ground than she had been that day in the barnyard.

"I know I'm taking a lot for granted," he said without preamble, "but I want you to do me a favor."

She waited, eyeing him cautiously.

"I've been on the phone to a man in Columbus who's coming down here in a day or two to buy some of my birds. Told him he could have his pick of what's left— ten birds for five hundred dollars, and forty bucks apiece for all over ten."

"Oh? Does that include the hundred-and-fifty-dollar one you offered me?"

"I want you to explain it to Ming—so she'll know it's all right. The money's hers, but she'll have to make it last for a month or two—so tell her not to let George Peabody get his mitts on it."

"You're leaving town?"

"Yeah. I'm catching a bus tonight."

"I see. It's none of my business what you do, Mr. Campbell, but would you mind telling me why you can't go out there and explain it to your daughter yourself before you go?"

"Because I'm a coward, Libby. No other reason in God's world." Mase's eyes left hers for the first time since he had entered the room. He looked out the window, at the maple trees red and yellow in the schoolyard, at a little girl in a fuzzy red hat who was trying to hold her skirts down in big-girl fashion as she hurried home against the October wind.

"Well! You're honest, anyway." She wanted to send him away. Maybe she would have if he had called her Miss Dean.

"I've got to . . . see a fella about a business deal," Mase said. "That fire last night wiped me out. But I know if I tell Ming I'm leaving she'll get a lot of wrong ideas—cry and carry on—Sara, too. I just don't want to go through it, that's all."

"No, you don't want to go through it. You want me to tell her because I won't mind if she cries and carries on when she finds out her father sneaked away without even saying good-bye."

"That's not it," Mase said sharply. "You don't understand——"

"You mean I don't understand that Ming's going to think you're running off to find that other man who was with you in the bank robbery?"

Mase scowled, his already raw face reddening.

"I'm not stupid, Mason," Libby said, more gently now. "That's where you're going, isn't it?"

"It doesn't make any difference where I'm going." Mase took a sheet of notepaper from his pocket and laid it in front of Libby. "This is the breeder's name. Will you do what I asked you?"

"I don't know." Libby took a deep breath. She looked up at Mason. "What about the nene geese? And

125

the bluebirds? And the painted quail and the thousand finches flying loose in an aviary as big as a house? Did they all burn up in your barn last night, too?"

"No!" The veins in his neck bulged. "I'm coming back, dammit—what's the matter with you!"

"You won't come back. Not to the birds."

"So to hell with the birds," he shouted. "Birds aren't important. You told me that yourself."

"What about Ming?"

His hand came down on her desk . . . *bam!* . . . like a cleaver. His face was contorted. He lifted his hand, clenched it. She thought he would hit her, but she didn't flinch. She stared into his eyes. Slowly—almost entreatingly—his hand opened. He let out his breath.

"I'm coming back, Libby. I'm not running away. I'm coming *back!* Will you please get that through your head? I'd wade through blood for Ming—do you understand that?"

"But Ming wouldn't want you to wade through blood. Don't be so dramatic, Mason."

"Don't be so dramatic?" He looked as though she had tapped him lightly between the eyes with a ball-peen hammer.

"Well, I don't know what else you'd call it," Libby said impatiently. "If you really thought anything of Ming you'd go down to Marion tomorrow and get a job in the factory. Or to Columbus. But no—that wouldn't fit your picture of yourself, would it? You've got to go tearing off across the country trying to find forty or fifty thousand dollars all at once. And I'll bet you don't have the faintest idea where to start looking."

He glared at her.

"Do you know what I think is the matter with you, Mason? If you don't mind my telling you."

He stared at her like a man hypnotized.

"You've never had any fun. You work like a demon and you fight like one—but there's nothing in between. You don't know how to relax and take it easy and laugh with people and just have a good time. When tensions build up in you, there's no outlet for them—until you sock somebody in the jaw, or perhaps hold up a bank."

"Is that a fact!" His tone was biting, but his eyes were not quite steady. For the first time since she had known him, Libby was able to push her own gaze deep into those fierce blue-silver eyes. She gained courage.

"It's all extremes with you, Mason. Win the Silver Star, rob a bank, spend ten extra years in prison rather than inform on the man who betrayed you. Even your birds—they've got to be the best in the world; you've got to win all the prizes at the bird show, start right at the top and go on from there, otherwise it's no good."

As she talked, Libby had time to wonder who was the more amazed—she or Mason Campbell. She had never thought any of this out before today. She wasn't even sure it was true. But the conviction grew in her that it *was* true, that she had intuitively picked up the right key. She had it in the lock now and was turning it, and in a moment the closed door which Mason Campbell kept between himself and the world would swing wide open and she would see him as he really was.

"If it hadn't been for that bird swooping down out of the sky last night, you'd have killed a man—and then everything would have been finished."

"No—I wasn't going to kill him."

127

"You don't know what you were going to do, Mason. You might have shot him. What if the sheriff had jumped on you—how do you know you wouldn't have shot him, too?"

Mase stared at her. His face was naked.

"Isn't it strange," Libby said, "that a bird saved you from committing murder? If you were a religious person you might almost think that God had something to do with it—a tiny bird, the symbol of peace, dropping from the night sky to rest on your gun barrel."

She felt her eyes burn. "And even if you don't believe in God, Mason, maybe you should believe in your birds. Ming told me how they started you on a whole new life in prison—and now one of them has made it possible for you to continue that life.

"But that isn't good enough for you, is it?" She shook her head in sudden anger. "You lost some of your birds —so now you're going to wipe them *all* out. Sell them to that man in Columbus. To hell with the birds. Mase Campbell's an all-or-nothing guy."

She stood up and turned her back on him and walked to the nearest window.

Mase said nothing. She stood at the window for what seemed a long time, staring with unseeing eyes into the sunny schoolyard. She grew uncomfortable. Had he perhaps simply walked out of the room—so quietly she hadn't heard him leave?

She turned her head—and looked straight into his eyes. He hadn't moved from the spot by the desk. He was just standing there, looking at her, his face completely open and unguarded.

128

"I thought you didn't care anything about birds." He sounded almost stupid.

"I don't! I care about Ming. And I suppose I care about you. Oh, not in any personal way," she added quickly. "But as I'd care about anybody who had a wonderful dream and the potential for realizing it. It's such a waste, Mason. It just makes me sick!"

He stretched his lips over his teeth. Not a smile.

"I never thought about it that way," he said in the same slow, stupid tone.

She bit her lip. He was like a man waking from a deep sleep. But was he really waking up? She thought that was too much to hope for. People didn't change that fast. And besides—it frightened her. This man's life was not her responsibility. She had no business trying keys in his locked door.

He pulled out a pack of cigarettes, lighted one, shoved pack and lighter in his pocket. She started to tell him he couldn't smoke here, then was tempted to remind him, sarcastically, that a gentleman would offer a lady a cigarette, too. But she said nothing.

He smoked silently, consuming the cigarette in long deep inhalations. It even shows up in the way he smokes, she thought. She wanted to tell him not to inhale so deeply, that it wasn't good for him. He looked around absently for an ash tray, then snubbed his cigarette in her potted geranium.

"I always thought I knew how to have a good time," he said, frowning at her. "What'd you mean by that crack?"

"Nothing. Nothing!" She was beginning to feel desperate.

He stared at her, his head slightly lowered, peering at her in a kind of dumb perplexity.

Like an ox, she thought. He gets an idea in that single-track mind of his and you can't shake him off it with dynamite!

"You might be right," he said, his voice slow, stumbling, stupid. "It feels like you said something important —but I just can't . . ." He spread his hands. ". . . I can't get hold of it—what it is."

"Well . . ." She felt a loosening inside her. Something slid away and something else slid in to take its place. As though blocks of steel were moving in grooves . . . *click* . . . this one moved down to a place that was right for it . . . *click* . . . another one moved easily and powerfully to an ordained position, interlocking somehow with something else. And there was suddenly more room inside her and it was easier to breathe.

"I usually go home and have a cup of tea after school," she said. "Would you like a cup of tea? And we can talk some more if you want to."

He stared at her as though she were speaking Chinese.

"Come on," she said. Her heels clacked loudly on the hardwood floor. "My car's out back." Her coat was downstairs in her locker and she decided to leave it there. She didn't want him to go wandering off on his own. Not right now.

CHAPTER TEN

It was nearly six o'clock. She had made tea—real tea, serving it from her grandmother's silver teapot. Mason drank three cups, handling the fragile Spode china as gingerly as canary eggs.

She was glad her apartment, all three rooms of it, was clean if not entirely neat. She wondered what he thought of her spindly Duncan Phyfe antiques, and the books, and the piles of professional journals and literary quarterlies she never quite caught up with.

He had taken off his jacket. The soft blue shirt, open at the neck, was becoming to him, she thought. His shaggy hair, so relentlessly combed at the school, was once again falling over his forehead, curling behind his ears. He looked more like himself——

But he didn't look the same. The impassive, stony expression had been wiped from his face. His eyes—those chilly blue-silver eyes—were puzzled, full of doubt.

"My bus leaves in thirty minutes," he said, scowling at his thumbnail as though he had just discovered it.

131

"Oh! I thought it was later." Her voice trailed off.

"I'm not going to be on it."

"Oh? Well, I'm glad you . . ." Her mind and tongue wouldn't work together. She wanted to say the right things—but it was almost impossible for her to speak at all.

"There's another one at midnight. I want to talk to you first. But I'm having a hard time getting started."

She held her cup and saucer tightly and sat very still and looked at the top of his head. Even the hairs of his head are strong and alive, she thought. In a few years he'll start to go gray, and maybe bald, but it won't make any difference.

She stood up, setting her cup and saucer down with a little crash.

"Well, I don't know about you," she said briskly, "but I'm hungry. Will you sit right here and wait while I run down to the market? Do you like steak?"

"Sure."

She grabbed her winter coat and hurried downstairs and out to the car. *"Sure!" That's all he says. Not, "Don't go to any trouble," or the other inane things people say. He's a very hard man to get used to.* Her mind was busy with him all the time she was gone.

"I thought this might do us both good." She pulled the tall rectangular bottle out of her grocery sack with a unnecessary flourish.

"Scotch whisky?" They were standing in the bright kitchen. Libby hadn't taken her coat off yet. He picked up the bottle, inspected the label. "I haven't had a drink for almost sixteen years."

"Why?"

"Well, liquor's pretty scarce in prison. . . ."

"I know, but I mean since you've been out?"

He shrugged. "Just didn't feel any need for it."

"Are you afraid you're an alcoholic?"

He looked at her, eyes sharp and wary. "No."

"Afraid you might relax and tell somebody your secrets?"

He grinned, mirthlessly. "Maybe." He peeled the foil off the top. "Want anything with yours?"

"Just water." She broke out a tray of ice cubes and then watched him mix two Scotches-and-water. He made them just the strength she would have—and it seemed natural and proper that he should be mixing the drinks in her house.

She broiled the steaks, and they ate—both with surprisingly good appetite. And then they had coffee. And then they had another drink.

"So you think I'm an extremist," he said, returning after three hours to the conversation that had brought him here.

"I didn't say that." She laughed. " 'Extremist' has all kinds of political connotations—I said you have a tendency to go to extremes."

"Yeah. I've been thinking about it. And I believe you're right." He squinted through his glass at the light. "I wonder what makes a guy be that way."

"Different things, I would imagine—for different people. It isn't wholly a bad quality, you know, Mason. Most of the world's great achievers have quite a bit of it in them, I'm sure."

"Yeah, I can see that." He sighed. "But they know when to ease off a little—bend with the wind when they have to."

She nodded. It would be better to let him talk, she thought. If he would just keep talking. He might find his own truths. She could never tell them to him. Because her truths wouldn't be his truths. And they shouldn't be. She was suddenly and for perhaps the first time very keenly aware of that.

"Why did you say I don't know how to have a good time?"

"Oh . . ." She was embarrassed. "I don't even know now what I did mean. I was just saying whatever popped into my head."

"Sure. But there's truth in anger as well as wine."

She met his eyes. For some foolish nonunderstandable reason she felt like crying. How could she have been so presumptuous!

"Would you like another drink? Sit still—I'll fix them this time."

She made the drinks. And then she sat quietly and listened to him talk. He talked about the Army and about his dead wife and about his dead father. She was sure it was the first time he had ever talked about either of them. He talked about Ming. The words came slowly in the beginning and then faster and faster, a torrent of words. He ran out of cigarettes. She gave him the pack she had bought at the market and stuck in her pocket. He was pleased. She fixed him another drink. It was ten o'clock. He talked about Ming, his voice tightening—and then easing, and it was all right again. He talked about his birds. And about the wild birds. And about the ineffable grace and beauty of birds. And the adaptability of birds. And the companionship of birds. And the independence and the obstinate willfulness of birds. And back again and again to the beauty of birds. Always this unexpected thread running strongly through all his talk: the beauty of the living bird.

She could only listen. She had thought he raised birds the way a hog rancher raised swine—for what he could get out of them. And now, listening to him, she realized that he raised birds the way an artist painted birds, and for much the same reasons. The aesthetics of birdkeeping? Would that be too strong?

"But you're saying that's not enough—aren't you?"

His question startled her. She had been listening to him, but listening sometimes for what he was *not* saying. And she had been for the moment content that he was apparently content.

"You say I ought to learn how to relax and take it easy, or maybe play golf or some damn thing or even go out and get drunk—anything to blow steam off."

"Well, I . . . didn't mean that exactly. I was thinking more of *people*. That you don't seem to relax and have a good time with *people*."

"You think I'm antisocial?"

"Oh, I don't know, Mason. What does antisocial mean, anyway? It's just a word—a psychologists' word. I used to be impressed with all that jargon, but now I'm beginning to find that when you try to dig into it you come up with a handful of air. The words are hollow. They don't really mean anything."

135

"Yeah?" It was his turn to be surprised. "I've always kind of felt that way myself, but I thought it was just another one of my antisocial tendencies."

She giggled. She would never tell him that the words had only begun to sound hollow to her in the past few hours.

"Part of it might be because I went to the Army so young. I was trying to act like a man before I knew how to act like a boy."

He had this disconcerting habit of reaching backward across minutes of conversation and picking up broken threads. A single-track mind, she had called it a few hours ago. But it wasn't single-track at all—it was multi-track, and the difference between him and most people was that he remembered what was on each track and where it was going. And he didn't let any of his trains get lost.

"But it's probably a combination of things," he said musingly. "And maybe it's just my nature. Environment isn't everything—I learned that with my birds. Two of 'em can come out of the same nest and one will be a cheerful happy bird, singing all the time, and the other'll be moody, contrary, a scrapper. Some birds are just naturally mean, and you can't change 'em no matter what you do."

That ran counter to most of what she had been taught —at least as applied to schoolchildren. "The myth of the well-adjusted bird?" she said, smiling.

He got to his feet in one of those quick effortless moves that always caught her unaware. She was afraid for a moment that he was leaving.

"Use your phone?"

"Of course." She looked up at him, and stopped being afraid. He was a different man—literally a different man! Where was the tight-faced, hostile, desperately committed stranger who had walked into her classroom that afternoon? Was it only the liquor that had loosened the knots? She didn't know. But she was full of hope —hope that this new face might be his true face. And why not?

He was dialing. He looked over his shoulder at her and grinned. To her immense dismay, she felt herself blushing. And as she tried vainly to control it, the heat spread from her face to her neck. She picked up a magazine and bent her head over it. She felt giddy, as though stricken suddenly with fever. He was talking on the phone now but all she could hear was the rush of blood in her own ears. She thought if Mason Campbell took that midnight bus—well, she'd just probably go right along with him.

Ming hung up the phone and turned a dazed face to her Aunt Sara. "He's with Miss *Dean!* Said he might be late and didn't want me to worry."

"Why, I think that was real thoughtful of him," Sara said comfortably. "What are you getting all up in the air about?"

"I'm not getting up in the air! But it's almost eleven *now*. What do you suppose they're *doing*?"

"Why, I suppose he's helping her wash the blackboards. What else would a thirty-seven-year-old boy and a pretty schoolteacher be doing in the middle of the night?"

"You have a very peculiar sense of humor," Ming said.

"I'm *serious*. He sounded so funny . . . I'll just bet you he's been *drinking*."

"Why, that devil! Next thing you know, he'll be smoking cigarettes and wanting to drive the car."

"Oh, you're just a riot," Ming said coldly. "My father's a very unpredictable man, Aunt Sara, in case you don't know it. I'm worried about him."

"Of course you are." Sara gave Ming a reassuring hug. "I was worried about him too, till you said he was with Libby Dean. And now I'm not worried at all. Don't you see?"

"Well . . . maybe. But he hasn't looked at his birds all day, and that's just not like him."

"Your daddy's been looking at those birds so long, he's forgotten there are females in this world who don't wear feathers and lay eggs. I'd say Libby Dean would be about the best thing that could happen to him."

He got home long after midnight. Ming heard the car in the driveway. She could hear the motor stop, and then she couldn't hear anything else for the longest time. And then her father entered the house, banging the door behind him, putting lights on, walking around, opening the refrigerator door, pouring a glass of milk, whistling, talking. *Talking?* But he was. And it dawned on her that he was talking to the birds in the dining room. She hoped he hadn't uncovered them and waked them at this hour. What was he saying? She couldn't hear— just the raspy resonance of his voice.

Then his step in the hall. Past her door. And now he was singing. Half under his breath—but singing. She had never heard him sing before. He was no Ray

Charles, that was sure. But he wasn't so bad either. His rough-edged voice hit the notes right:

"When autumn weather turns the leaves to flame,
One hasn't got time for the waiting game ..."

She hadn't thought he would even *know* "September Song." She snuggled down under the covers. It was all right. He was probably drunk, but it was all right. She fell asleep and dreamed of a bright golden bird poking its head out of the blackened ashes of the barn, shaking itself clean, and then flying straight to her shoulder, where it sang a strange, soft song she had never heard before.

CHAPTER ELEVEN

At nine the next morning, Sheriff Sam Dunbar's black Ford with the big gold star on the door pulled into the driveway. Ming was eating breakfast. Her father hadn't come down yet, and Sara had told Ming to be quiet and let him sleep.

Watching through the dining-room window, Ming saw the sheriff get out of his car and stroll toward the ruins of the barn. He didn't even glance at the house. Ming left her half-eaten oatmeal and hurried outside. It was a wonderfully crisp, clear morning. The burned smell of the barn—so ugly yesterday—was blending now into the other smells of autumn. But the birds were there in the ashes, Ming knew, and every time she thought about them, it made her sad.

"Daddy around?" The sheriff touched the brim of his gray hat.

He can't be going to arrest him, Ming thought. He wouldn't be so polite.

"I think he's still asleep."

Dunbar lifted his eyebrows.

"He was up late. He's been working awfully hard."

"Hate to disturb a working man's rest," the sheriff said. He didn't grin. "But I'd sure like to talk to him."

Ming felt a flutter of fear. She nodded, and raced back to the house. Maybe he *was* going to arrest him! You couldn't tell with Sheriff Sam—he always came at you sort of sideways, and she remembered how polite he had been the day he subpoenaed Uncle George to that court hearing when the tractor company went bankrupt.

"He's in the bathroom, shaving," Aunt Sara said. "What's Sam want?"

"I don't know," Ming whispered. "He says he wants to talk to Daddy."

Sara grimaced. In her experience, Sam Dunbar's arrival at the Campbell farm invariably spelled trouble.

Mase came into the kitchen. He smelled of shaving lotion. His eyes were bright and clear as mountain springs. He smiled at Ming, and at Sara.

"Birds look good," he said. "Appreciate it."

Ming returned his smile. But her mouth felt stiff. He was so handsome and clean and full of life this morning. And the sheriff was out there by the barn. . . .

Mase drank a cup of coffee, not hurrying; then put on his suede jacket and went out to talk to the sheriff. Ming watched from the window. Mase walked across the yard with his head up and his shoulders square. He didn't walk fast and he didn't walk slow. He walks the way a man *should* walk, Ming thought—as though he owns a piece of the world and will always own it, regardless of sheriffs and fires and tongue-tied daughters.

She saw the men nod at each other. The sheriff began to talk immediately. He talked a long time. Mase shook his head. Ming could see him try to interrupt, but the sheriff gestured vehemently and talked faster and Mase stood there and listened. When the sheriff stopped for a moment Mase said something and then the sheriff made another speech. At least that's how it looked to Ming. The sheriff was trying to talk her father into something and her father was saying No.

They walked slowly around the ruined barn, and for a while Ming couldn't see them. But when they came back in sight the sheriff was still talking, and her father was listening. He wasn't shaking his head so much. He was nodding—reluctantly, doubtfully—but nodding. Ming felt a sharp lump form in her throat. If Sheriff Sam talked her father into going with him . . . what then? How long before she would see him again? But it might be worse if he *couldn't* talk him into it. It would be bad either way. Bad. Bad. Bad. If only Mase hadn't pointed that gun at Bert Bradley. She hated Bert Bradley with every ounce of her being.

They were walking toward the house now, her father so tall and wide-shouldered, the sheriff squat and heavy, his big gray hat tilting as he looked up at Mase.

"I'm going into town with Sam," Mase told her, poking his head in the front door. He was smiling. He didn't look scared or worried—but that didn't mean anything because he never looked scared or worried.

She nodded, licking her dry lips.

"I'll only be a little while," he said. "Anything you want?"

Just you, she wanted to tell him. Just come home again—that's all I need. But she could only shake her head, drawing a long breath, trying to smile.

He winked at her and was gone. She watched the

142

black Ford swerve out of the driveway and then disappear around the bend in the country road.

"He'll be all right," Sara said. "They're not going to do anything to him—not for showing up that flannel-mouthed Bert Bradley."

Ming was not so easily consoled. Bert Bradley was a deputy sheriff, and her father had knocked him down and then pointed a gun at him. Even if the sheriff *had* said he was suspended . . . it might not mean anything. Maybe Bert Bradley had sworn out a warrant for her father's arrest . . . maybe . . . maybe a million things. You just never knew what men were going to do . . . they'd say one thing and then do the exact opposite. Men were not very dependable, Ming thought. They didn't know, themselves, what they were going to do until they started doing it—and there was no way in God's wide world that a woman could ever understand them.

Ming waited tensely for two hours. She was so nervous her stomach was beginning to hurt. "You're making yourself sick," Sara told her. "Why don't you check the birdies in the hospital cage—your daddy'll be home when he gets here, and you'll feel better if you keep busy."

The "hospital cage" was simply a big cage Mase had covered with a sheet and surrounded by table lamps. The heat from the bulbs warmed the interior. He put a thermometer inside and instructed Ming to keep the temperature near ninety. "Heat's the best medicine for a sick bird," he had said. And apparently he was right. The seven remaining little patients all seemed much improved. They had lost their dull puffy look, and two

143

were singing. She hadn't had a chance to tell her father yet that she had recaptured four good healthy canaries yesterday of the dozen or so that had winged their way out of the burning barn. And she had left several cages with their doors open in the yard, hoping that more of the birds might be tempted to exchange their precarious freedom for security.

She moved the lamps away a little, to bring the temperature down gradually. Then she cracked a few sunflower seeds for Bully, who dearly loved to eat sunflower seeds and would sit hopefully on her finger as long as he thought there was a chance for another one. Sara had gone upstairs for a nap. She had probably lain awake last night till Mase came home, Ming realized. Aunt Sara was a puzzle—she'd get all in a tizzy about some little thing that didn't amount to a hill of beans, but let real trouble strike and she'd calm right down and be the steadiest person in the house.

Ming was tired too—not sleepy tired, though. She didn't think she'd ever be able to sleep again until her father came home and told her everything was all right again. She fussed over the birds and played with Bully and perhaps drifted off into a daydream of happier times. Finally she put Bully back in his cage, and when she wandered over to the window, there was the sheriff's black car with the gold star on the door, sitting right in the driveway.

But no sign of the sheriff and no sign of her father. Frightened, she rushed outdoors. Gazed wildly about— and saw her father standing by the chicken run, one hand resting on the wire, absorbed in the antics of the stupid scurrying clucking hens.

"Hi!" She ran toward him. She felt hollow with apprehension. "Where's the sheriff?"

He turned and held out his arms. And for the first time in her life she ran directly to him and into his arms. He hugged her tight for a moment. When he released her she looked up at him. She thought he was smiling but she couldn't see him very well.

"Darn it! I don't know why I always have to *cry!*"

Gravely he offered his handkerchief and she wiped her eyes and blew her nose. And when he put the handkerchief back in his pocket, his short suede jacket swung open and she saw the star pinned to his shirt pocket. She pulled his jacket open. It was a heavy silver star with round knobs on the points, and in the middle of the star it said "Deputy Sheriff" in big letters and the name of the county underneath in small letters. She looked up at him in astonishment. She couldn't move. The world hung suspended around her.

"You . . . ?"

"Yep."

"*You!*"

"Me." He grinned.

"How . . . ?" She couldn't get her breath. The world had sprung into motion again around her. Everything going so fast. The chickens scratching and clucking like maniacs, the wind blowing the grass, the sun dancing on the bright shiny star.

"He said he needed a deputy—an interim appointment, he calls it. I thought he was crazy, too. But the funny thing is, there's no law against an ex-con being a deputy sheriff—as long as you can make a bond, and Sam had that all fixed up with the bonding company someway."

145

"I can't get it through my *head!*"

"I can't either," Mase said soberly. "And that's a fact."

"Will you *like* being a deputy sheriff?"

"It's a good job for a lazy man." Mase rubbed his jaw. "Hell, I don't know, Ming. At first I said No. Couldn't see myself as a policeman. But there are cops and there are cops, Sam said, and you don't have to be a Bert Bradley." Mase paused and looked searchingly at his daughter. "What do *you* think about it.?"

"Gosh, I don't know," she gasped. "But you know something?"

"What?"

"I'm awful proud of you! And you should be proud too!"

"I don't know yet if I can be proud of being a cop," Mase said slowly.

"My gosh, I never even *heard* of a man coming out of prison and being offered a job as a deputy *sheriff!*"

"Plenty other people may feel the same way—only they won't be proud, they'll be madder'n wet hornets."

"Well, just let them be," Ming said stoutly. "As long as Sheriff Sam wants you, what do you care!"

They walked toward the house, side by side.

"The thing that swung me," Mase said, grinning, "is I'll be able to sneak home and look at my birds once in a while."

Ming ran ahead of him. She felt like running clear to town and dancing all the way back. She spread her arms. She thought she might even be able to fly. She turned and faced her father.

"Wow! You're going to be some *kind* of a deputy sheriff!"

146

CHAPTER TWELVE

All through the summer of that year, Fred Sander had been seeing ghosts. Tall, wide-shouldered men disappearing around corners. Chilly-eyed men peering at him from windows. While crossing State Street one day in the fall, he had to leap for his life when a truck ran a red light—and in his fleeting glimpse of the driver he recognized the back of Mason Campbell's head, the way the neck and head came up off the shoulders.

Shaken, he retired to a nearby bar.

I'm bugging myself, he decided after his third double shot. It wasn't Campbell. None of them had been Campbell. But someday it'll be Campbell—if I'm not dead of ulcers or heart failure first.

If I just knew where his family lived . . . I could phone them, pretend to be a reporter, find out when they expect him home. He ransacked his memory, trying to recall every scrap of conversation he had ever had with Campbell. He thought he remembered Campbell once mentioning Ohio . . . but he wasn't sure. And it was no help, anyway. There must be ten thousand Campbells in Ohio.

Finally, in desperation, he slugged down two more stiff drinks, and from a pay phone in the Loop he called the warden of the Florida State Penitentiary. Gave the name of a national magazine. Said they had stumbled on the Campbell case while searching old newspaper files— thought it might hold some interest for their readers. Wondered if Campbell was due for release soon, or would the warden permit them to send a man down there to talk to him?

It was cold in the phone booth and his ungloved hands were numb, but he could feel the sweat trickling from his armpits down his ribs.

"Sho, sho . . ." the warden was chuckling, surprisingly cordial. "But you're a little late. A little late . . ."

A humming in the wires. Or was it in Sander's head?

"What's that? Can't hear you!"

"I said he's gone home." The voice pierced Sander's eardrums. "Expiration of sentence."

Sander, terrified, glanced over his shoulder.

"Ah . . . could you give me his home address?"

"No, I couldn't," the faraway warden said. "And wouldn't if I could. Mase Campbell's done his time— and I reckon if he wants to talk to any reporters he'll get in touch with you fellers on his own hook."

"But . . . look, we're prepared to offer him a good sum of money. You'd be doing him a real favor, Warden."

"Sho." The warden snuffled through his nose. "Mase Campbell never did take too kindly to folks doing him favors—as you'll find out when you locate him. Good luck to you!" And the warden hung up.

148

Sander walked Chicago's cold windy canyons for an hour. The pulverized debris of the city blew against his face like emery dust, and it gradually sharpened his despair to a kind of frantic high resolve. At three o'clock he entered another phone booth and did what he should have done ten years ago.

Called a reliable private detective agency.

Laid it on the line.

"I want to locate a certain party," Sander told the agency man. "I don't want him to know anything about it. I don't want you to know who I am. Now where do we go from here?"

"Routine matter," the agency man said. "Put two hundred dollars cash in a plain heavy envelope and address it to me personally. Or send it by messenger. Enclose a slip of paper with the number three-three-two on it. From now on that's your code number. Three-three-two. Got it?"

"Yes. But how do I know I'm not just throwing the two hundred down a hole?"

"It's the chance you take. You can have a signed receipt, or you can have anonymity. You can't very well have both."

"All right. Then what?"

"Then call me and give me as much as you can on this party. We'll make a start for the two hundred. In seven days call me again. If we haven't located him we'll need more money. And I'll tell you right now, mister, if it's a cold trail it may run into dough."

Sander hesitated. They could milk him from here to eternity on that system. But he had no choice.

"All right." He felt the phone booth suddenly become warmer and more comfortable.

"Don't forget your code number. Every time you call. Otherwise you'll get no information. This is strictly for your protection, mister."

It wasn't a bad system, at that. In fact, it was nearly foolproof both ways. At worst he stood to lose a few hundred bucks, but the agency could never finger him even if they wanted to.

And when they located Campbell—what then?

Well. He didn't want to think about it. Maybe he could hire . . . No. He would have to do it himself and he didn't want to think about it, but he knew that when the time came he would do it. One way or the other he would do it.

He shivered.

What a horrible thing it was! His secretary slopping around the office, all wrapped up in her asinine neurosis. His salesmen, in and out, always crying. Everybody thinking they had problems, and if they only knew how safe they were and how happy they ought to be! They were civilized people living in a safe, warm, civilized world. He had been part of that world yesterday. Now he was roaming fearfully in a jungle. And there was a cat in the jungle—nine feet tall, with eyes that could see in the dark. He didn't know where the cat was and the cat didn't know where he was. But the cat was looking for him.

"How'd you like to go to Chicago with me?"

"*Chicago?*" Ming looked up from her homework. She was studying at the dining-room table. It was only

150

six o'clock, and the birds had not yet been covered. She liked to be near them. When a geometry problem refused to make sense she could rest her eyes and her poor tortured brain on a happy canary. She thought it helped.

"That's where they're holding the National this year. I'm going to enter a dozen birds. First I was going to ship 'em, but Sam said I could take three days off—so I'll drive up. Hate to ship 'em anyway."

"That's *wonderful!*" She hadn't mentioned it, of course, but her father had been so busy with his new job these past weeks—and with Libby Dean—that Ming had wondered if he was perhaps losing interest in his birds.

"You mean it? Can I go with you?"

"You might miss a day or so of school."

"Oh, I can make it up! Which birds are you going to take?"

"Well now, we'll have to look 'em over and decide. Which ones do you think?"

"Oh, I wouldn't be able to tell!" She glanced shyly at him. Was he teasing her? He didn't appear to be. He looks so fine in his uniform, she thought. It was gray, with black trim. And when he went out he wore a wide-brimmed Stetson hat. When he was on duty he was supposed to wear the heavy belt and the big black revolver. She had never seen him take it out of the holster, and she noticed he often didn't wear it even when he was supposed to.

Sheriff Sam had dropped by one day and told her that her daddy was already a very good deputy. "Of course— he never makes any pinches, but maybe it's because trouble seems to stop before it gets started when he's around. We had this bunch of tough kids—supposed to be tough kids—hanging around Ben Angelino's road-house out on the lake road. Nobody could handle them. I sent your daddy out there one night and those kids were nice as pie. Been that way ever since. Mase has a way with kids—they like him and respect him, and I'll tell you, Ming, it ain't the easiest thing in the world today to command respect from some of these long-haired kids."

"Well, I'm a long-haired kid, myself," she had told the sheriff, and he had said Yes, he guessed she was.

"I figure we might take six cocks and six hens," Mase said, squatting before the row of cages which had been stacked along one wall of the dining room ever since the fire. It was as good a place as any to keep them, Sara had agreed. She simply rolled the rug back and let the seeds fall as they would, swept the floor twice a day, and the rest was up to Mase and Ming.

"We've got fifteen healthy hens here, and if we have a good season next year, we'll be back in business."

"Will you sell the ones you take to Chicago?"

"No, no. Can't afford to sell our breeding stock. What we want to do now is convince the breeders up there that we've really got the red canary, and then next fall they'll be knocking our door down trying to get birds—we hope." He grinned over his shoulder at Ming.

"But what if the birds don't win?"

"Then we've just got some nice Red Factor canaries. But we'll never know till we exhibit them."

"You know—I never really felt excited about it be-fore." She joined him in front of the cages. "But it's just like . . . like betting on a horse race, isn't it? You breed the birds and raise them, and you think they're good. But then you have to enter them in the show, and

152

from then on it's out of your hands—it all depends on whether some judge thinks they're good, or whether some other breeder has birds that are better."

"That's the story when you're breeding any livestock for exhibition," Mase said. "When you're breeding for glory or for big money. But if you've got faith in your stock, you don't let a judge's opinion influence you too much. You keep following your own ideal and maybe in the end the judges gradually switch around to your way of looking at things. Exhibiting's only one phase, anyway, and you shouldn't put too much importance on winning."

"Hah! But you want to *win*—now don't you?"

"Sure." Mase glanced sideways at her. "But we might lose. You've got to be ready for that, too."

"Okay, Mr. Philosopher." Ming laughed. "But you're not going all the way to Chicago expecting to lose, and I don't care what you say!"

"We."

"Huh?"

"*We* are going to Chicago. *Our* birds are going to win."

"Oh!" She turned her head away from him and pretended to study the birds in front of her. "I used to wish you would give me just one bird for my own," she said, a hitch in her voice. "Maybe I shouldn't have said that."

"I don't know why not," Mase said strongly. "When you're in partners with somebody you've got a right to say what you think."

"Okay." She turned and smiled at him. "Partner."

It took them days to select the twelve show birds. The

153

clear, hard-feather birds were the reddest and most spectacular, but it was important that the other breeders see the frosts and the variegates and the dimorphics, too, so they'd know what the whole line looked like. "We want to try to win in a couple of different classes so they'll know they're not freaks," Mase explained. "The biggest danger we've got to face," he warned her, "is that the judges may not let these birds in the Red Factor classes at all. If they throw 'em in with the dilutes or miscellaneous . . ." He shook his head darkly.

Ming only partly understood what he was talking about, but she was beginning to dread these shadowy, arbitrary, all-powerful judges.

For the males, they finally settled on three clear reds, two frosts, and a variegated red-mahogany—and they picked out six assorted hens, two of them the striking pink-and-white dimorphics that had first caught Libby Dean's eye.

"This has got to be the prettiest canary in the world," Sara said, holding up one of the show cages in which Mase was giving the birds their training. "If he had a crest, he'd look just like a cardinal."

"Like a *cardinal?*" Mase looked first at Sara and then at Ming and then at the bird. "Like a *cardinal!*" He stared at the canary till the bird started to shift its feet nervously. "So help me if he doesn't! And all this time I was so sure I had a mutation. . . ."

Sara put the cage down, keeping a wary eye on Mase.

"But what I might have had was a cardinal cross—a cardinal-siskin-canary cross. That could explain the dark underflue *and* the color!"

154

"So where's the mystery?" Sara said. "If you had a cardinal with the canaries——"

"I never *had* a cardinal with the canaries. But I used to put my birds outside a lot, especially the hens to rest 'em between nests. The place was lousy with cardinals. I've heard about birds mating through wire but I never really believed it—never even considered it.

"Naw, it's impossible." He shook his head. "They gave up on the cardinal-canary cross twenty years ago. And why would a wild cardinal go to all the trouble of mating with a canary hen through the bars of a cage?"

"Maybe he wasn't popular with the lady cardinals. Or maybe he couldn't see very well or something," Sara said helpfully.

"Dammit, Sara. What'd you ever come up with an idea like that for? All these years I've had it figured out—nice and pat—and now you've gone and put a cardinal in the woodpile."

"So maybe it wasn't a cardinal. Maybe it was some other kind of a red bird."

"Maybe it was an Irish setter. I'd rather settle for the cardinal if it's all the same to you."

"Will it make any difference?" Ming asked. "At the show, I mean."

"Who knows?" Mase shrugged. "No, that's not right—it'll make a difference. If they think it's a cardinal cross, it'll make a big difference." He rubbed his jaw, frowning. "If I knew for sure they were cardinal crosses I'd enter them that way . . . something new . . . might knock their eyes out. But this way, I don't know . . . I don't know," he repeated slowly. "Seems like the only

155

fair thing is to enter them as a new variety—ancestry unknown."

"I hope I haven't spoiled anything for you, Mase." Sara was close to tears. "Just because they look like cardinals to *me*—Lord, that doesn't mean anything."

"It means a lot—and I'm grateful to you for opening my eyes. Maybe I knew all along there was something odd about these birds, but I kept culling out the worst of them and breeding for better canary conformation— same as I'd have done if I had known there was cardinal blood. . . ." He kept shaking his head as the full significance sank in. "But the underflue is *recessive*—you can't get away from that. So how could it show up in a first cross?"

Ming felt a rising sense of exasperation. That bird certainly didn't look like a cardinal to *her*. A cardinal was built different—bigger and coarser, and with a red bill, for Pete's sake!

Her father wasn't wishy-washy about other things— why was he so full of doubt about his own achievement in this, the one field where he was really an expert?

She didn't know. But she was suddenly afraid he didn't really expect to win in Chicago. She was afraid he was going up there the way a country boy rides the bus to New York for a tryout with the Yankees. Playing choose-up in the pasture was one thing, and the big leagues were something else, and the country boy stood a good chance of being laughed right out of the ball park.

CHAPTER THIRTEEN

Ming and her father drove to Chicago in a new Ford wagon lent to Mase by the dealer in Blairsville. "He called it a demonstrator," Mase said, grinning. "I guess it's one of the fringe benefits of being deputy sheriff in a small county."

They made it in a day's easy driving, but then the city traffic slowed them down and it was almost nine when they pulled up in front of the hotel where the National Cage Bird Exhibition was being held. Entries would close at eleven, Mase explained, and then the judging would begin early the next morning and be completed around two in the afternoon, when the show would open to the public.

Ming helped him carry the two roped stacks of cages into the crowded lobby. The bird people had taken over this hotel for the weekend, there was no doubt of that. The lobby was full of feathers and bird song. And bird talk. She saw two ladies with large green parrots perched nonchalantly on their shoulders. The ladies were talking and so were the parrots, and for a moment she had the uncanny feeling it was a four-cornered conversation. She wheeled involuntarily at a piercing wolf whistle.

"Just a fresh cockatoo," Mase told her. "Pretend you're with me and maybe he'll go away."

You'd think he'd been doing this all his life, Ming thought, enviously. I know darn well he's never been in such a madhouse before.

As they pushed through the lobby she saw heads beginning to turn. At first she thought it was her father they were looking at. He stood taller than anyone in the room. He needed a haircut, and a shave, and in his old suede jacket he looked—she supposed—just a shade on the rough side for a first-class Chicago hotel. Not that she was any bargain, herself, in her rumpled skirt and old cardigan. But the curious eyes were sliding off him, and off her, and fastening with an almost audible snap on the birds they were carrying.

Mase sauntered along, glancing from right to left occasionally, his pale blue-silver eyes unconcerned. No one spoke to them, although everyone else seemed to be speaking to everyone else. She wondered if it was because they were strangers, or because her father's eyes, even when he was feeling friendly, just didn't invite people to step up and speak to him.

They followed a string of signs into a huge ballroom, part of which was curtained off. She received an overwhelming impression of birds—thousands of birds, all kinds of birds, row on row of nothing but birds—and then the curtain blocked her view and she was standing with her father at the end of a line leading to a counter marked ENTRIES. Even here, there were caged birds all over the floor. Bustling men with badges proclaiming their official capacity as stewards were constantly on the run, lugging cages behind the curtains, but it looked to Ming as though they were fighting a losing battle. Most of the birds in view were canaries, many of them orange and various shades of near-red, but nowhere did she see a bird whose color approached the deep pure red of her father's birds.

While they waited a man came into the ballroom from the lobby and stared directly at Mase, narrowing his eyes a bit, hesitating—you could almost see his mind working, Ming thought—and then walked slowly up to her father and said, "You wouldn't be Mason Campbell by any chance?"

Mase nodded.

"I'm Sampson Remarque." The man stuck out his hand, grinning now.

"Well, well," Mase said. Ming had never heard her father say well, well, before. He was grinning, too—the rare beaming grin that made him look like a boy of twenty.

"Harry Wheeler told me somebody just walked in with the reddest canaries in Christendom," Sampson Remarque said as they shook hands. "And I told Cyn—that's my wife—told her I'll bet that's Mason Campbell."

Sampson Remarque was an erect slender man, around sixty, with crew-cut white hair and bland, hooded gray eyes. He was wearing an obviously expensive dark-blue business suit, and looked—Ming thought—more like a banker than a bird fancier.

Mase introduced his daughter. Remarque said something pleasant, and Ming found herself liking him. This was the man who had sent her father his first good birds. That had been a long time ago. And for all these years they had been writing letters back and forth, talking about their birds and probably about other things, and now for the first time they were meeting face to face. Men were always very careful to cover up their emotions, Ming had noticed. But this was an emotional moment. Old friends meeting for the first time. And they didn't know quite what to do about it.

"I . . . uh . . . had a little bad luck," Mase said, and he told Remarque how many birds he had lost in the fire.

Remarque shook his head, wincing visibly. "Seems like you've had enough bad luck for one man."

"Good luck, too." Mase smiled. "Got me a helluva partner."

Remarque smiled at Ming, and she wouldn't have traded places right then with Miss Teenage America.

Now there were only two people ahead of them in line. Mase eased the roped cages a few feet forward. Sampson Remarque glanced down at the birds, then quickly looked elsewhere.

"Come on!" Mase said, laughing. But his voice, usually so even, was strained. "I might's well find out now as later. Are they any good?"

Remarque knelt quickly, eyes intent, face impassive. "You know they're good." He glanced up at Mase, opened his mouth, closed it—then stood up, frowning. "They're good. They're good. They're fantastic. But . . ." He hesitated. Mase stared straight at him. "But what are they?" Sampson Remarque said.

"What *are* they!" Ming was indignant. "I thought that was a pretty stupid thing to say."

It was the next morning, and she had come from her own room in the hotel to Mase's. She hadn't slept as well as she had thought she would. She had awakened several times, momentarily bewildered and frightened. The room was so quiet. People sometimes complained that the country was quiet, but there were always night sounds in the country: a lonely owl hooting from the woods, crickets telling the temperature, tree frogs croaking up a rain, wind whispering secrets to the sycamore outside her window. Here in this city hotel there was only a faraway humming, nothing she could identify, nothing to reassure her that other creatures were alive in the land.

"Well, he didn't exactly mean it that way," Mase said. He had put on a clean white shirt, and he had shaved, but those were apparently the only concessions he would make to big-city fashion. "What he meant was I might run into trouble with the classifiers."

"Yes, but you knew that without him telling you."

"He was just trying to warn me not to expect too much," Mase said patiently. "Sampson's a hundred per-cent—so don't you be jumping to any wrong conclusions."

"I know." Ming smiled. "I guess us women always take things too personally. But he sure didn't go for your cardinal story, did he?"

"He sure didn't. And he's probably right. He's seen more hybrids than I've ever heard of."

"But he didn't seem to know what it *could* have been if it wasn't a cardinal—nor the other men, either."

"The main point seems to be that it doesn't matter too

much now—mutation or out-cross—the birds are all past the third generation, which makes them canaries regardless of how they got started." He stood up and shrugged into his jacket. "Let's see if we can locate that coffee shop and get us a bite of breakfast."

"Are you going to watch the judging?"

Mase shook his head. "I'm putting up a pretty good front, but I haven't got the heart for that." He grinned. "Anyway, we've got a couple other things to take care of this morning."

Her father, Ming realized as they walked through the lobby and entered the coffee shop, was already a sort of minor celebrity among the bird people. A dozen strangers called out to him, wishing him good morning or good luck.

"But they're not really strangers," Mase told her. "Over the years I guess I've written to a hundred different people, and they remember."

They remember you were in prison too, Ming thought. She had heard of other men coming out of prison and putting it all behind them—starting life all over again in a town where nobody knew their background. But with her father it certainly wasn't like that. Everyone in Blairsville knew all about him—and every one of these bird people knew or would soon know. Did it matter? She had to admit that it didn't *seem* to matter—and she wondered if maybe it wasn't better this way. At least they didn't have to worry about somebody finding out!

He didn't tell her what the "things to be taken care of" were. She tagged along incuriously, eyes and mind too full of the sights of Chicago to wonder much about where they were going. As they entered the revolving door of Marshall Field's she looked up at Mase in some surprise.

"Are you going to buy a suit?"

"Nope."

She wished he would buy a suit. Not that she was ashamed of him in his leather jacket, but the fact was you didn't see too many men walking the streets of Chicago in leather jackets. She just wished her father could walk back into that hotel wearing a suit of clothes like Sampson Remarque's. You'd really see some eyes pop then!

Mase put her in the lead once they got inside the big store. Told her to find the department where they sold the kind of clothes she liked to wear. And she found exactly that department, thinking he just wanted her to look, which would have been treat enough. But then he told her what she could spend. It was a lot of money—more than she had ever spent on clothes in her life. She stared at him, disbelieving.

"Forgot to tell you I collected insurance on my truck," he said, grinning at her. "Didn't even know I had it insured against fire till Royce Randolph handed me the check last week. And then your aunt Sara talked me into taking some of that old glassware of Ma's to an antique dealer in Columbus. Wasn't worth what she thought it might be, but it helped."

If for a fleeting instant, after she had finally grasped the reality of it, she wished she could have a whole day or three or four days to shop the city before making her choices, she realized that this would be expecting too much of any man. So she put her mind totally to the business at hand and within three hours had picked out a wardrobe. She wished Libby Dean could be there to help her. Or even Aunt Sara. But the blue-haired saleslady was almost as good, steering her tactfully away from a certain party dress and showing her why this particular cordovan loafer was twice the buy even at two dollars more.

Mase wandered off for a while. "Why don't you buy yourself a new sport jacket anyway, Daddy," she urged him.

"Might," he said. But when he came back he was still wearing the same old stuff. He was carrying a big box, though.

"What did you get?" She really wanted to show him what *she* had got, but the saleslady had convinced her it would be silly to carry all those packages when they could just as easily be delivered right to the hotel before four o'clock that afternoon.

"Well, I bought some underwear," Mase said in a low voice. Ming guessed he didn't want the saleslady to hear.

"Underwear? A whole boxful of underwear?"

"Well, no—I stumbled onto the pet shop while I was roaming around, and they had this real fancy house cage. . . ."

"You bought another bird cage!" She didn't know whether to laugh or cry.

Mase rubbed his jaw and looked embarrassed.

"I bet it's a dandy," she whispered. "And you're a dandy, too."

"We located him," the agency man said. "But you could've saved yourself some money if you had told us in front who he was."

"I told you who he was." The phone felt slippery in Sander's hand. Now that the waiting was over, now that it was coming in the next breath or two, he felt an odd reluctance to hear it.

"I mean *who* he was," the agency man said deliberately. "But maybe I understand now why you didn't."

Sander looked over his shoulder through the glass of the phone booth. He could see the attendant gassing his car. There was no one else in sight. "So where is he?" he said gruffly.

"Ohio. Little town called Blairsville."

Blairsville . . . "What's it near?"

"Forty miles from Columbus. Campbell's got a broken-down farm outside of town. Raises birds."

"Raises *birds*? You sure you got the right party?"

"No doubt about it," the agency man said smoothly. "Our boy held up the Farmer's Trust in Jacksonville back in forty-six. His rappy got away with eighty thousand potatoes. Course you didn't mention that little item."

Sander was tempted to hang up. That was the hell of it. Things never stayed simple when eighty thousand dollars entered the picture.

"It's none of my business," the agency said. "You paid your fee and you'll get what you paid for. And that's the end of it as far as I'm concerned."

"All right. What else?"

"He's a deputy sheriff."

"*What?*"

"Yeah. And don't ask me how come, because I wouldn't know."

"That can't be! There's something wrong here!"

165

"I wouldn't be surprised." The agency man sounded tired. "Look, mister—why don't you come into the office and we'll talk this over. Or I'll meet you someplace, if you'd rather do that. You sound like you need a little help, and I just don't think we can do any more business over the phone."

Sander hesitated. More than anything else right now he needed someone to take part of this load off his back. Mase Campbell a deputy sheriff! It made no sense whatsoever. But the habit of fifteen years was too strong.

"You're taking a lot for granted, buster." Trying to make his voice hard. "I don't need that kind of help."

"Maybe you don't and maybe you do." The agency man sounded bored. Also sounded . . . mocking? "Your friend's not in Ohio at the present moment, by the way."

"Well where *is* he?"

"I hate to be so blunt—but the fact of the matter is, you've already got more than your money's worth on this particular deal."

"All right, all *right!* I'll send you another two hundred. But I'm not coming to your office and you can just forget about that part of it."

"Look, mister. I'm frankly not interested in another two hundred. I think you need some protection and that'll run a little higher than two hundred. But I'm not going to shake you down; I want you to understand that. All I'm interested in is earning a decent fee and we'll discuss the size of it when I talk to you in person."

"No soap."

"Have it your own way." The agency man sighed.

"On second thought, I guess you did pay me to tell you where Campbell is."

Sander waited, not breathing.

"He's right here in Chicago."

The agency man's voice roared in Sander's ears—and then faded, as though Sander and the phone booth had been suddenly transported to outer space. "You'll probably be hearing from him. . . ."

"Now wait!" Sander cried frantically. "Wait!" He glanced over his shoulder—saw only the service-station attendant, idly polishing a windshield. "We can work something out," Sander whispered.

There were only a few stragglers in the hotel lobby when Ming and Mase came downstairs, and none of them seemed aware of the miracle that had transformed her from Miss Slop to Miss Sleek. Well, they'll notice back in Blairsville, Ming consoled herself—moving away from her father in a slight detour that would take her past the full-length mirror between the elevators.

And as she turned from the mirror she saw the strong set of her father's head, the restrained tension in his shoulders, and she realized with a flash of sickening self-condemnation that she had entirely forgotten what was waiting for him in that ballroom. Ten years' work, and the dream of a new life, hung on the whim of some crotchety canary judge—and here she was, strutting in front of mirrors, hung up on her own silly little pretensions!

They were almost at the ballroom door. People streamed past them, laughing, talking, busy with their own affairs. Ming grabbed Mase's big hard hand and squeezed it. "Good luck," she whispered. "Good luck! Good luck! But even if you don't win, it'll be all right. We'll try again next year—won't we?"

"Sure we will." He smiled down at her. And she saw that he meant it. Win or lose . . . they *would* try again next year. And it was all right. It was all right!

In through the door. Into a world of birds. And people. Lots of people. Looking at birds. Gazing at birds. Squinting, peering, staring mesmerized at birds.

First the rows and rows of parrakeets. Ming and Mase walked stolidly past them. Parrakeets were all right too—but not right now. And then the big hookbills, the parrots and cockatoos and macaws. Down this row and around the corner. Canaries now. Strange tall canaries standing in their cages like soldiers. "Yorkshires," Mase said. No time for Yorkshires now. And then big round canaries, plump as partridges. "Norwich," Mase said. And now trim sprightly canaries, green and yellow, brave and full of bounce. "Border Fancies," Mase said. They would come back later and look at the Border Fancies. Because here were the first cages with the flash of color—the deep oranges and the pinks and the chocolate reds—the only canaries Ming knew anything about, and it was like meeting old and beloved friends.

But they weren't red. None of them were really red. Not red like her father's birds. She saw ribbons on some of the cages. Blue ribbons and red ribbons and yellow ribbons and big rosettes that said FIRST, and SECOND, and SPECIAL. But nowhere in the long long rows of Red Factors did she see a single bird that belonged to her father.

She was afraid to look at him. She kept leaning over to read the ribbons and the little signs. DEEP-RED ORANGE, one of them said. And FIRST PRIZE. A pretty bird. Yes. But not like her father's birds.

Mase hadn't said a word. She stole a swift glance at him. He was frowning.

"Hey, there!" Sampson Remarque came scurrying up the aisle. He had a gray suit on today and he looked too cheerful. "My, but you look nice," he said to Ming.

I'll bet he's a salesman, she thought. But he knew how to make you feel better when you were feeling terrible, and she couldn't help smiling at him.

"Well now, Mason," Sampson Remarque said. "I've been watching for you—wanted to catch you before you started prowling around here by yourself."

"Appreciate it," Mase said. "They threw 'em out, eh?"

"Well now, not exactly," Sampson Remarque said. He was obviously agitated, looking over his shoulder for someone. "Over here, Florrie!" he shouted. Fifty heads turned to stare. Ming felt herself blushing. Then a great galleon of a woman in a silk print dress bore down on them under full sail. "Mrs. Florabelle Blennerhasset," Sampson Remarque announced. "Best Red Factor judge in the country, bar none, and you better believe it."

Mase nodded—rather respectfully, Ming thought. "I've read your articles——" he began.

"Pah! Anybody can write articles," she said. She had an astonishing voice, clear and pure as a mezzo-soprano's —but she used it very recklessly. "Birds are the thing— not articles about birds."

Mase nodded again, cautiously.

"I had to wrong-class your birds," she caroled—as

169

though it were nothing, Ming thought, hating her—as though it were just some little thing she had to do every day.

"Hated to do it—but really no choice in the matter. No choice at all."

Mase sighed. He wasn't a sighing man, but Ming heard him sigh then.

"Can't put birds like that in a red-orange class," Florabella Blennerhasset went on vehemently. "Might as well ask me to judge apricots with lemon yellows!"

They were moving down the aisle, guided—pushed would be closer, Ming thought—by the always cheerful Sampson Remarque.

"Okay," Mase said indifferently. "Where'd they end up—Miscellaneous?"

"*Miscellaneous!*" Florabelle Blennerhasset was the only person Ming had ever heard who could make a complete aria out of one word. "Well! Is that all the faith you have in your birds, young man?"

"Take it easy, Florrie." Sampson Remarque waved a soothing hand. "This is Mason's first show, you know, and we want him to come back for another one."

"Of course you do. Of course you do." Florabelle was unruffled. They turned a corner, coming into an open area in the center of the ballroom. "There are your birds, Mr. Campbell," the famous lady judge said, waving a studiedly casual hand. "I established a new section for them, with the agreement of the show manager, of course. Otherwise they wouldn't have been eligible for anything in the Red Factor——"

The rest of her words were lost as Ming raced across the room to the small raised stage. There were perhaps

170

thirty birds on view. She saw one of the Yorkshires, and a parrakeet, and even a tiny hummingbird in a glass cage—and she saw her father's birds, all twelve of them in a proud line.

"Your number-one bird got BEST-IN-SHOW," she heard Sampson Remarque say as the others came up behind her. "I mean he beat everything in the hall. The Yorkie and the rest of them are Division winners. But there's nothing here to touch your birds, Mason."

"And I do hope you won't mention that philandering cardinal again," Flora Blennerhasset cried. "Oh, Sampson told me all about it, and I reject your theory utterly. These canaries are positively a mutant Red Factor variety —*not* double dilutes as Sampson thought—*not* cardinal crosses. These are *red* canaries, Mr. Campbell. The first in the world. And I want to thank you from the bottom of my heart for giving me the opportunity to so declare them."

Florabelle Blennerhasset was smiling, and then there were tears in her eyes, and then she was crying.

Ming stared in amazement. But she remembered some of the things her father had told her. For forty years canary people had been pursuing their elusive red singer. Now the search was over. To Florabelle Blennerhasset the moment of fulfillment had been a great moment, like Balboa sighting the Pacific, like a medieval zoologist finding a unicorn in his garden—and it would be entirely beside the point to argue that a canary was hardly in a class with an ocean or even a unicorn. Because each of us has his own ocean and his own unicorn, and a comparison of absolutes is always impossible.

CHAPTER FOURTEEN

"It may not fit the popular image," the agency man said. "But a private investigator is basically a law officer—that's the principle our outfit operates on, and I think you'll find most of the good ones do."

Mase nodded dubiously. He wasn't convinced—there were too many other reasons a private dick might have dealt himself into this kind of a game.

"It smelled bad from the start," the agency man said. "These anonymous clients are always hiding something besides their names. But that part of it was all right. Where it started to be not all right was when I back-tracked you to that Jacksonville job. It didn't take a genius to figure out that my number three-three-two and your onetime partner were the same guy."

"So?"

The agency man was in his fifties, fat, short, untidy. He looked like an unsuccessful used-car salesman. Saggy creased face, shrewd tired brown eyes. And Mase was beginning to believe him.

"So I tried to smoke him out of his hole, but it looks like I blew. He panicked on the phone and agreed to a meet. And then I suppose he cooled off and started using his head. He wouldn't have had to call many hotels before he found you in this one."

"And you came down here to tell me this just because you want to give me a break?"

The agency man grinned. "I wanted to see what you looked like. I already don't like number three-three-two. And it's against my principles to sit still and let somebody I don't like take pot shots at a deputy sheriff."

They were at a table in a corner of the hotel bar. It was nearly five o'clock. Mase had been paged and had come from the ballroom to find the agency man waiting for him in the lobby.

"Why don't you tell me who this joker is? I'll turn it over to the city cops and they can pick him up."

Mase shook his head. Was it possible that this private dick was not a private dick? That he was maybe an FBI dick? Or an insurance dick? Was it possible that this was one last complicated effort to trap him into revealing the name he hadn't spoken for fifteen years?

"I don't know what name he's using now," Mase said slowly. "He'd be hard to find, even if I wanted to turn him in. And what would they charge him with? Statute of limitations on the bank robbery ran out years ago."

"You got a point. Maybe that's why he's so scared of you. You're the only man in the world he's really got a right to be scared of."

"But he doesn't have to be scared of me. That's all over with. All I want now is to live in peace."

"He'll never believe it," the agency man said. "A scared man is dangerous. You got a gun?"

Mase shook his head.

"Why don't you go down to the Cook County sheriff's office and borrow one? You may need it."

"Maybe I will."

"Want me to stick around?"

"No. But I appreciate it—your coming down here and all. If you ever need a favor in Ohio, I hope you'll let me know."

"You may never get back to Ohio." The agency man stood up and put out his hand. "But good luck."

Mase watched him go. The bar was nearly empty. Bird fanciers, by and large, didn't spend many daylight hours in cocktail bars, but Mase saw a few familiar faces, and as they met his eye they smiled and nodded.

Nice people, Mase thought. Friendly people, most of them gentle people. A friendly gentle world it had been till an hour ago, and now suddenly he had been ripped out of that world and tossed back into a world of greed and fear and criminal violence. A world where cold dangerous men would commit murder for profit, where desperate frightened men would commit murder for no reason at all. A world where you sometimes couldn't tell the cops from the robbers. A world that Sampson Remarque and Florabelle Blennerhasset had never made. That Ming Campbell had never made.

Ming! What about Ming? Assuming the worst, assuming that Fred was gunning for him—it seemed almost impossible that he could know Ming by sight. Which meant that Ming would be safe as long as she stayed away from Mason Campbell. But how to arrange this without telling her the truth?

For the moment, anyway, she was safe in the ballroom, where Sampson Remarque and his wife were giving her a short course in aviculture. Mason left his table and walked up to the bar. He ordered a Scotch and water, and thought immediately of Libby Dean. But this was not the time to think of Libby Dean, or of Ming, or of anything else except Fred Simpson.

If I were Fred, Mase asked himself, what would I do? Remembering now that I'm scared because I think Mason Campbell has come to Chicago to kill me. Or maybe to shake me down and then kill me.

Would I try to buy Campbell off? No. I wouldn't be able to trust him. Would I believe Campbell if he told me he didn't want to kill me, didn't want anything from me? No. I sure wouldn't believe that—not if I were Fred, I wouldn't.

So what would I do? Well, my first thought would be to run away and hide. But I'm forty years old now, and I've got money and position, and I don't want to run away and leave it. So the only alternative then is to get Mason Campbell before he gets me. And how will I go about doing that little thing?

I won't walk right up to him and shoot him. Because I don't have the stomach for that kind of action. And besides I don't want to get caught. Which means I won't go to his hotel. Because he might see me before I see him, and it would also be very hard to get away with murder right there in the hotel.

So what I'll have to do is get him *out* of the hotel, get

175

him to come to a certain place where I'll be waiting for him and there won't be anyone else around, and then I'll shoot him in the back.

"Give me another one of these," Mase told the bartender. He felt much easier. Felt almost relaxed and good. And it wasn't the whisky. It was just that he knew now where the danger lay and he would be ready, and in the meantime there was nothing to do but wait and try to stay loose.

He sipped his drink. The Scotch tasted good. This was a good comfortable bar. Warm. Soft music. Enough light to count your change. He wished Libby were with him.

When the call came he would have to tell Ming it was from Sheriff Sam Dunbar. Someone in the Chicago jail that Dunbar wanted him to talk to. Not the best story in the world, but it would do. Ask the Remarques if they would take Ming under their wing till he got back. Sampson would wonder, of course. Tonight was the Awards Dinner. Mason's canaries would be the big item, and Sampson Remarque would wonder what could be more important than that.

And then there was the matter of the two pairs he had put up for sale. A breeder named Paul Bascomb had offered him five hundred dollars for the number-two male and a dimorphic hen. Mase had swallowed and then opened his mouth to say Yes, when Sampson Remarque had smoothly interrupted with a reminder that winners were usually sold by sealed-bid auction. Bascomb had shot Sampson a dirty look and asked if he was Campbell's business manager. But Mase had gathered his wits by then and announced that he would be selling two pairs, and the high bidders could pick up their birds when the show was over.

Sampson had told him later that he might get over fifteen hundred dollars for the four birds and had urged him to go ahead and sell eight or ten. It would kindle terrific competition for next year's show, and even though he would never get prices like this again, the red canary would stay in the hundred-dollar bracket for several years and Mase would be the only breeder producing them in quantity.

But Mase had decided against selling more than the four. He was already short of males, and some of those he had were untried. This way he could with luck raise maybe a hundred young birds next season. Say he sold fifty at a hundred dollars a copy. It would be a good start. And the third year, even if prices were off a little, he would have three or four times as many birds for sale. . . .

He was starting to build a new barn in his mind when it came:

"Call for Mason Campbell!"

The bell captain directed him to a booth.

As he picked up the phone he was surprised by a searing flash of anger. He had thought the anger was dead. But now . . . now . . .

"Mase?"

"Yeah."

"You won't believe it, Mase. But this is Fred Simpson."

No, I don't believe it, Mase thought.

"I saw your name in the paper," the voice went on.

"Just now. About the new canary." Simpson was having trouble with his breath. Mase waited, said nothing.

"Look—I know you hate my guts. I don't blame you, Mase. But when I saw your name in the paper I just decided it was time to get straight. If it's possible, Mase. I mean—I expect you want to kill me and I don't blame you, Mase. But honest to God, I want to try to make it right with you. If you'll give me a chance. Will you give me a chance, Mase?"

He sounded like a little kid—like a little kid who had maybe wrecked his best friend's bike and then lied about it, and was now pleading for a chance to make amends. And of all the possible ways Fred Simpson might have come at him, this was the one way Mase had not anticipated.

"I'll give you half what I got, Mase. And I got plenty, believe me. But it's no good to me. I'm dying of ulcers and a guilty conscience. If you put a bullet through my head it won't make a whole lot of difference. That's the way I feel."

You're a liar, Mase thought. And if it wasn't for that private dick I might have believed you.

How could he talk to him? And what was the use of talking to him? Mase was almost strangling in his own bitter juices.

But he did talk to him. Forced a few meaningless words out. Tried for a moment to tell him that he had no need of vengeance. And realized quickly that this would never work. Simpson was scared—that was the thing to remember. Simpson would believe only what he wanted to believe. But Simpson didn't know that Mase

had been warned—and the thing to do now was go along
—keep him out in the open where he could see him.

He agreed finally to meet Simpson in a Rush Street
Club. Mase didn't know anything about Rush Street.
Simpson said it was kind of a high-class honky-tonk row
—but this was a nice club and there would be lots of people around and it would be protection for both of them.
Mase asked him to come to the hotel where they could
talk in his room—or in the bar. But Simpson wouldn't
go for it, and Mase knew why and didn't argue with
him.

When he hung up and turned around, Ming was standing there in the lobby waiting for him. She had heard
him paged, for the second time that evening, and now
she was wondering and she was worried and maybe a
little frightened.

Mase told her the lie about the sheriff. She seemed to
believe him, or at least pretended to believe him. Then
he had to see Sampson Remarque and tell him the lie
and ask him to look after Ming for a while.

Remarque was instantly alert, questioning Mase with
his eyes.

It was the one thing a man with a record couldn't get
away from, Mase thought. People didn't exactly expect
the worst, but they were more or less ready for it. And
it didn't change anything that in this case they were right.
Or did it? Was there an aura of criminality, or a smell,
or a force of some kind, that attended these excursions
into that other world? Libby had known immediately,
that other time. And now Ming and Sampson Remarque
had both reacted with that same quick doubt.

I'm probably just the world's lousiest liar, Mase thought, shrugging and turning away from the concern in Sampson's eyes. He went up to his room for his jacket, opening the door suddenly and reaching in to snap on the wall switch but not entering the room till he was sure it was empty.

He wished he had a gun. But he wasn't going to the Cook County sheriff's office to borrow one. And maybe in a way it was just as well. He didn't want to kill Fred Simpson. At first he had thought he would have to kill him, and it had seemed easy and natural to kill him. But now he was beginning to hope that there might be another way. He didn't know what it would be, and he found that he couldn't even think ahead and try to figure out what might be the best way. It suddenly began to seem unnecessary and almost incomprehensible that he should kill a man.

The trouble, he realized clearly, was that the two worlds were for the first time in his life beginning to slide into each other, to overlap, to contain the same people—and, perhaps most important, to contain the same Mason Campbell.

It was very strange. Always before, even a few minutes ago when he had sat in the bar planning his tactics, the two worlds had been entirely separate. Mason Campbell, bank robber, and Mason Campbell, birdkeeper, had been two different people. The bank robber didn't know Ming Campbell, and the birdkeeper had no connection with Fred Simpson. He had been both men, but never simultaneously. He had jumped from one to the other as the occasion demanded, and had managed quite successfully to keep the two Mason Campbells and the two worlds they inhabited separated one from the other.

But suddenly it was no longer possible. Fred Simpson had pushed his way into the birdkeeper's world, and the birdkeeper was now moving, unarmed, into the bank robber's world. And the two worlds kept overlapping more and more, like two circles sliding together. First there were two separate circles and then a confusion of curved lines and intersecting arcs that didn't even look like circles and then the two circles matched up and there was only one perfect circle and he was in it and Fred Simpson was in it and so was Ming and so were the birds and Libby Dean and Blairsville and the Florida prison and even the bank job. And there was only one Mason Campbell. That was the most unsettling thing. There was no other Mason Campbell he could turn Fred Simpson over to.

He rode the elevator down, went past the desk with the key in his pocket, out into the cold neon-flickering street. He felt peculiar—that was the only word for it. He wasn't as sure of himself as he had been an hour ago. But he felt . . . what was it? Better? Did he feel better? That seemed a stupid thing to say. He didn't exactly feel *better* but he felt *wholer*—if there was such a word. More whole. More of a piece. Bigger? Not bigger. But solider. Because two Mason Campbells had become one Mason Campbell? Maybe. He wasn't used to analyzing himself this way. He felt all right, though. There was no doubt of that.

He took a cab instead of bothering with the station wagon. It was a short ride, just across a bridge and down a garish, cheerful street lined with bars, nightclubs, restaurants, what-have-you.

"This is a pretty fancy joint you're going to," the driver informed him. "None of my business, buddy, but in case you're from out of town—you ain't exactly dressed for this joint."

Mase thanked him and gave him a dollar tip. It didn't look so fancy outside, but there was a doorman who said, "Goodeveningsir," and there was a flight of stairs going down, and a hat-check girl whose eyes widened slightly, and a cigarette girl dressed mainly in long black stockings who gave him a cheerful impudent grin.

"You in oil or cattle, pardner?" the cigarette girl asked, blocking, perhaps accidentally, the narrow doorway that led to where the action was.

"Birds," Mase said, smiling.

"Birds?" She looked up at him, her eyes appraising. "Well, this isn't Birdland, but make yourself at home." She swung the cigarette tray out of his way, and he stepped down two thickly carpeted steps into the club proper.

The cabdriver had been right. A fancy joint. A long room, severely modern, decorated only with fantastic writhing silver-gray pieces of sculpture—which weren't sculpture at all, Mase saw, but pieces of driftwood, polished and shaped by sun and water. The driftwood and the cool gray light gave the place a kind of shimmery, underwater feeling. A fancy joint, yes, with a long bar on the far wall and a four-piece combo playing soft jazz on a small bandstand and the rest of the room densely populated with well-dressed handsome people, eating

182

and drinking and talking and laughing, but all in a quiet, expensive way.

Mase scanned the room. He didn't see Fred Simpson. He walked slowly across the room to the bar. He kept his eyes open—though it seemed very unlikely that Fred Simpson would try any rough stuff in a place like this.

The bar was not crowded. He took a seat at the near end, empty stools on either side of him. The bartender —young, sharp in his white mess jacket—frowned.

"Scotch and water," Mase said mildly.

The bartender poured the drink, still frowning. Mase laid a dollar bill on the bar. The bartender looked at it, and then put a large, stiff cardboard check face down in front of Mase. He turned it over. Scotch—$1.50.

A very fancy joint, no doubt about it. Mase laid another dollar on the bar. When he looked over his shoulder to survey the room again, he found quite a few people regarding him with varying degrees of interest. But he didn't see Fred Simpson.

So I should have bought a suit, he thought. Poor Ming must think I look like a slob.

"Mase!"

He turned his head. Slowly, cautiously.

Fred Simpson was standing right behind him. Bald, poached-egg eyes, grooved anxious face. Older than he should be—thinner, weaker, tireder, scareder, hollower, emptier. The husk of Fred Simpson in a four-hundred-dollar suit.

"I've got a corner table," Simpson said. "We can talk."

Mase sat down across from him. There was a party of youngsters at the table behind him, very busy with each

183

other. No one else close enough to worry about. Their waitress was perkily noncommittal. Mase ordered Scotch. Simpson ordered crème de menthe and fresh cream—half and half.

"It's all I can drink these days," he explained. "Stomach's killing me."

When the waitress had gone, Simpson tasted his drink, made a face, then laid his manicured hands flat on the table and looked Mase full in the eye for the first time.

"For once in my life I'm going to be honest, Mase. Maybe it's stupid, I don't know. But I . . . I found out I can't handle this any other way."

Mase waited.

"You didn't come to Chicago to kill me, did you?"

Mase shook his head.

"I know you didn't. I knew it when I saw the story in the paper about that canary. But I almost killed you, Mase. I had it in mind that I had to kill you before you killed me. And if I hadn't seen the story about the birds, I think I would have done it. Or tried to do it."

The birds again. If there are guardian angels—Mase was thinking—mine wears feathers. He lit a cigarette.

"Well, say something! I know you hate my guts. I don't blame you. But I want to try to make it right, Mase. Will you believe that? So help me God, I'm telling you the truth."

"You can't make it right, Fred. I'll say that before we go any farther. But if you're telling me the truth—and I guess you are—then that's absolutely all I want from you. Nothing else. You've got nothing to worry about."

He stared at Simpson, and Simpson met his eyes for a moment and then flushed and looked away.

184

"Mase, I feel terrible. None of it's any good—the money and the freedom and the rest of it." He tried to smile. The whole top of his head was furrowed as he peered up from under his eyebrows at Mase. His mouth quivered. "Mase, I want you to have half of what I've got. I'll cut you in for a full partnership. . . ." Talking faster now, eager. "We'll twist this town's tail, Mase. I've got the money and the know-how, and you've got the drive and the guts. You can own half of Illinois in five years. . . ."

Mase shook his head.

"Now Mase, I'm leveling. I'm worth a lot of money. A lot more than you think."

"I don't doubt that," Mase said. He thought briefly of the money, how it would be to have money, what he could do with the money and what Ming could do with it. He thought of the run-down farm and the burned barn and the birds in Sara's dining room.

"It wouldn't be any good, Fred. But I appreciate your offer."

"Appreciate my *offer!* What's the matter with you, Mase! The money's here. It's yours. You did fifteen years in the can for it. Now take it and quit this messing around."

"I don't want it."

Mase grinned. The amazing thing was that he *didn't* want it. And he understood dimly why he didn't want it. The money would change everything. The birds he bought with the money would be cheap birds and the new barn would be a cheap barn and what the hell fun would there be in it?

"Are you a deputy sheriff, Mase?"